Night of the Vigilante

CW00670049

David Overland.

Big thanks to Mary as always.

Big thanks to Sam for ideas, plot suggestions and general wisdom as well as providing a constant ear.

Big thanks to Stan, Steve, John and Gil as well as all the others for inspiring this and making my childhood so much more interesting.

Big thanks to those rare souls in the comics industry who've remembered that they need to send the elevator back down.

Massive thanks to all of you who are prepared to give Indy authors a go.

For Sam and Ben

He's got a black hand-gun, with a red plastic clip over the trigger, he pulls off the clip with some difficulty whilst I watch, then he points the gun at me. I can see his hand shaking from twenty feet away but it's excitement that's making his voice shake.

'Give me a reason freak.'

See, I'm sure that's not by the book, they go on courses and stuff, learn protocols surely? This isn't 'Call of duty'; it's not a computer game.

I should just leave, I can get away easily but my mouth is in the wrong gear. 'A reason for what?' I just can't help myself sometimes.

'Don't get funny with me freak; face down hands on your head.'

Was it that funny? 'I've done nothing wrong.' I tell him calmly.

'You attacked those men!' He blurts, his gun still doing a jig on the end of his arms.

'Those four attacked another who's since legged it. Why would four law abiding citizens be walking around with two golf clubs an iron bar and a baseball bat in the middle of the night?'

He shoots and for me it's like time freezes, I can almost see the bullet, I've got the angle of the barrel, the movement of his hands, I know where it's going and its going to miss (by about a mile!)

I lean back getting myself further out of the way just to be sure then I'm on him before he realises, I pull the gun from his hands and throw it onto a garage roof on the other side of the lane.

Then I grab him by the collar pushing him into the wall of bricks behind him.

'You know I'm getting sick of this,' I try for a snarl but the mask makes it sound more like a hiccup. 'Look at them!'

I drag him to the four men unconscious on the floor. 'Look!'

'I'm a police officer you can't . . .'

'Why would four law abiding citizens be carrying two golf clubs an iron bar and a baseball bat around with them on the wrong side of town in the middle of the night?' I repeat my perfectly reasonable question.

Suddenly he's properly outraged, his moustache squirms on his lip as he snarls, 'it is not for the likes of you to hand out law and order! We're the . . .'

'The what officer?' I interrupt getting hot under the collar myself now, 'there's thirty seven of you trying to do the work of eighty, your superiors have allowed government to decimate your force. The streets aren't safe my friend . . .'

Apparently a declaration of friendship from a masked and

costumed vigilante is the worst of insults. 'It is not for the likes of you . . .' he pauses trying to get his mind and mouth into the same gear, he's properly outraged now, red-faced and the moustache is bristling. 'I AM THE LAW!' He barks, 'WE are the law.'

'And you have to sit in your offices filling out forms whilst the streets around you become more and more unsafe.'

That does it, he punches me again and again. To me it's like a toddler having a tantrum, little podgy fists with no weight or power behind them, his face screwed up like a cabbage patch doll.

This is one of the things that's cool about power, you can't be hurt, you can't be touched.

Don't get me wrong, he's a lot bigger than me, an inch or two taller and much bulkier. I imagine under normal circumstances he'd be a right handful in a fight but I know from experience that none of these blows will even leave a bruise.

He stops eventually, panting, sweating and a frankly alarming shade of red.

I lean forward, getting my masked face an inch or so from his. 'Do you want to know what happens when the law fails officer?'

He's got no answer this time.

'I'm what happens!'

I'm gone in an instant, that's another part of the deal that's cool. I can't fly and I don't (regrettably) have a web line but let me tell you a secret.

Climbing is about strength, you see those guys on youtube scrambling up skyscrapers with their fingertips. The stronger you are, the easier it is to lift your own weight and that's what climbing is mostly about.
I can get up the side of most buildings in seconds, I just need my fingertips, I'm no natural climber but climbing comes easily with strength, especially great strength.

I leap up onto a wall to my right, the facing corner of the building behind is black with shadows. My costume is dark and I disappear in a moment. The eyes of my mask are covered by what looks like thin red Perspex. It's military tec known as sharpfilm, they use it in night vision goggles and periscopes, it allows me to see clearly in the dark.
I leap from the garden wall to the corner of the house behind it. It's Victorian and brick, child's play and I'm on the roof in seconds.
Now if this was a comic there would be a full moon, low behind the chimneys. I'd pause for a moment in front of it and stare moodily down at the city but I'm in no mood for

brooding and there's no moon anyway just smog.

I race across the rooftops and I'll admit that this side of it all is pretty cool.

There's a late night chippie below and I'm starving. The costume is basically motorcycle leathers with modified gloves and boots. I take the jacket off and reverse it, it's just a black leather jacket now. I put the mask in one pocket and the gloves in another and shin down a drain pipe.

Angie in the shop tells me I'll have to wait for the chips, then she tells me about her life as my chips cook and bubble behind her.

Angie tells me that she's forty three and if this is true then she's had a really hard life, I'd say she's closer to sixty but I'm not going to tell her that.

She's thinking of moving back in with Tony but she's not sure, he's got a part-time job in the market so he's handy for fruit and fresh veg. but he snores and walks in his sleep and he supports Everton.

I tell her that the snoring and sleep walking can both be solved by a good slap but supporting Everton could be the deal breaker.

She laughs as she entombs my chicken and mushroom pie and freshly cooked chips in rolls of newspaper, then she tells me to take care as she gives me my change, short changing me by a quid which I'm too polite to mention.

Outside after checking that nobody's about, I'm up the side of the building and blowing my chips on the roof as I stare moodily down at the city, brooding over my supper.

It's not the police's fault, they're in an impossible position and most of them are decent people. Bravest thing I've seen in recent times was a PCSO dive into a burning car to pull out what she thought was a child. The driver was outside the car screaming that her baby was in the back. The copper was a lot closer so got there before I could and she dived into the flames. Straight in, no hesitation, you should have seen her. Turns out her baby was a Chihuahua, I got the copper out and ran her to the hospital.

She's the only person who's seen my face but I doubt she noticed, I just lifted her up in my arms and ran and ran.

They're doing the hardest of jobs in the worst of times with well below the absolute minimum number needed to do it properly.

Lena in the flat next to mine works in a shop, she told me that the shareholders told the senior managers in the store to make a deal with the junior managers in the store. The junior managers in the store would get extra wages providing that they stopped all complaints about staff numbers from those beneath them.

The shareholders then got the senior managers to cut staff numbers to the bone in order to cut costs and maximise their profits. When the workers at the sharp end cried out the junior managers swept it all under the carpet and insisted on business as usual.

Problem was what made the shop special was its customer service, this evaporated as the staff diminished and then before you know it the business folds.

Lena's standing to be a councillor. She'll get my vote but I'm not sure I can see what she'll be able to do.

I have a sneaking suspicion that the stores business model is pretty much standard practice everywhere that you look nowadays. Everywhere you look the system is broken, nothing is able to work as it should because nothing is resourced properly.

The United Kingdom endured a dozen years of austerity, then the extremely divisive Brexit referendum then the Covid pandemic and where I live, the country is on its knees.

And I am seeing all of this for the first time, I'm coming at it fresh, as an outsider and it is, all of it, new to me.

The chips are too hot and the pie not quite hot enough, the food is okay but my head is reeling with it all because all of this, all of it, is new to me.

I can tell you my name and I can tell you my age but only because I've been told myself.

I have a flat and a car and a job as well as a super powered alter ego but I have no idea how I got them or who I really am.

Let me explain

The official version is this one, I volunteered with a pharmaceutical laboratory developing a potential cure for MAS, a rare but extremely unpleasant muscle wasting disease. Rather bizarrely the company in question was bankrolled by the military.

Something went wrong, something in my blood reacted with the chemical and I had some kind of seizure of the brain. Now it seems that the only person who wasn't surprised by this was an army doctor called Grey, he was there, supposedly, to ensure that the military were getting value for money but he took charge at this point.

It's not known exactly what happened then as the lab staff were escorted from the building. When Hillary James the senior doctor who ran the lab found out she contacted the military as she had a contact, a General no less, she rang him and then all hell broke loose.

A squad of soldiers and specialist police stormed the lab. It turns out that doctor Grey was under investigation with the army anyway and had placed himself in the lab without the army's knowledge or consent.

As the soldiers and armed police reclaimed the lab Grey drew his gun and fired upon them and was killed in the return of fire.

The police found that all of the written records had been burnt and the computers had been wiped. I was there alone and unconscious hooked up to a drip.

Because of the situation with Covid in all of the local hospitals, they made the decision to keep me there where I could be nursed by the doctors in the lab. Initially I seemed fine everything was perfectly normal and the only issue I had was temporary amnesia.

Over the following week however, weird things started to happen. Mitch the doctor who looked after me did CT and MRI scans and came to the conclusion that I'd had some kind of brainstorm (and that's not as cool as it sounds.)

The doctors who organised the experiment were extremely interested in the mechanisms behind hysterical strength. You know the kind of thing, when a woman who's only five foot two and slightly built is suddenly able to lift a car because her child's trapped beneath it.

There's loads of instances, its because we've all got reserves of strength that we never use but sometimes in an emergency we can access it. We're not talking about an adrenaline rush here, this is something deeper. Our own neural inhibitors generally dictate how much strength we can access and this is for our own good, it stops us breaking bones and tearing muscles. In addition if we ran everything at max our bodies would just burn out as our muscles became exhausted.

The lab wanted to see if there was a way that these mechanisms could be used to counter act MAS, the disease essentially attacked muscles tissue, weakening it progressively. Could these mechanisms be manipulated to enable the body to fight back?

The first stage would be get control of the neural inhibitors (which are unique to everyone) then to boost the subjects strength with a compound known simply as y54. Before you ask I have got no idea what's in it, neither had the lab, all they would say was that all of its components were natural, that is found in nature rather than cooked up in a lab.

It was the one component in the experiment that was provided by the military. Grey told them that the compound had shown promise in providing a temporary boost to strength and resilience and because they were bank rolling the whole of the project Hillary agreed to try it. The lab had their own compound called trysene so the first guinea pig (me) would get y54 and the second guinea pig Yasmin, blonde with freckles I met her once, would have got the trysene the month after.

In my case at least part of the experiment had worked, over the days I just got stronger and stronger. In the space of a week I no longer needed glasses, my hearing became excellent and I could run faster and jump higher than an Olympic athlete.
This was great but it didn't stop.
For another fortnight it continued. My appetite was insane, thousands of calories a day, I should have been the size of a house. I lived in the gym and the canteen and I just kept getting stronger and stronger.
Now all of this sounds great but believe me there's so much baggage that comes with it.
I had to learn how to do everything again, walking, running, jumping, how to grab and how to hold. All of a sudden my world is made of balsa wood.

Then without warning everything kicks off again, the lab's on the outskirts of a commuter town twenty miles from the capital. You know the kind of thing seventies new town a thousand shades of concrete and above all quiet.
Well its midmorning and suddenly vehicles are screaming to a halt outside and helicopters are in the sky. Armed soldiers

dash into reception screaming a dozen things at once. Now this time its Hillary that doesn't seem surprised, she comes into my room and puts an orderly called Mark in my bed. I put on his coat and badge and go down the back stairs with another orderly called Adam, more about him later, it's like it's all been planned.

There's an industrial estate behind the lab and a fast food place behind that. Adam has an old focus parked outside it and in no time we were miles away.

It took the military a day to realise they'd taken the wrong person and then photo fits started to appear on the news but the face wasn't mine, Hilary had deceived them in this also.

Now back to Adam the orderly, he is Adam Jacobs and he plays a large part in this story, not least because it was him that told it to me.

It was Adam who told me my name, gave me the keys to my flat and my car and the whole superhero thing was his idea. He pinched the sharpfilm when he was in the TA and bought the leathers and he came up with the name *Any-man* because I could be, just any man.

Yep the newspapers thought the same thing as you just did, so they started calling me the Vigilante and that's the name that's stuck.

It was Adam that reminded me that I was good with computers and he's right, machine code, binary and C++ I can remember all that perfectly I just can't remember learning it or what I did with it.

So Adam sets me up, according to him I had no family, I'd been through the care system as a kid and had been looking to settle down in London anyway. I'd volunteered for the work in the lab to get the money they paid in expenses. Now according to Adam, when the lab checked my details, they discovered that I'd been in quite a bit of trouble in the past but after confronting me Hilary accepted that I was just trying to make a fresh start and only needed someone to give me a break.

Now the lab need me to disappear there's no record of what's been done, they can argue that it was Grey who instigated the experiment and without notes or records the work can't be repeated. The army and the police have what they think is my photo, it was actually cooked up in photoshop so they're looking for someone who's never existed.

The lab has paid my rent for a year, to give me time to find a job and get settled and all I needed to do now is to keep my head down and not to draw attention to myself.

As I said the whole costume thing was Adam's idea, he'd been given a right kicking by a group of lads he'd known in night school, they just turned on him for no reason.

They put him in hospital for a fortnight and on crutches for six months, a year and a half afterwards he still has a bit of a limp. Adam dreamed up the whole costume thing so I could get revenge for him. He'd done so much for me so it was the least I could do, I beat the living daylights out of the four of them in the same car park that they done Adam in (he watched from the back of his Focus.)

Thing is it was so easy, we went for a pint afterwards and Adam said that the costume and mask would allow me to make a difference and hold onto my anonymity and he was right.

So it's all neat and tidy right?

Yep that's what I thought, Adam encouraged me to keep a blog, things I remember, things that strike me, a general record of what happens in my day. I don't see him much now just send him a copy of the blog every month.

The blog is apparently what you do with amnesia, you keep a record, it helps you to piece your memories back together. So I did just that and soon discovered that it was being closely monitored by three different I.P.'s no less, clever code, well hidden but I'm a computer expert remember.

So as of today I'm keeping two blogs, the official one and this one and believe me nobody is hacking into this one. Y'see I just don't buy it, any of it, Stephen Bishop is a name that rings no bells with me whatsoever, people call out Stephen in the office and I don't react, they have to shout or wave.

The face in the mirror is mine but I'm certain that it was never called Stephen then there's girls. Now don't get me wrong I like girls, I'm obviously heterosexual but Helen in the office is practically perfect, she's gorgeous, single and really friendly so how come every time that I talk to her I feel like I shouldn't? Like I belong to somebody else.

The office incidentally, is Hendrick's Computer Consultancy and William Hendrick is my boss, think of a skinny Boris Johnson but with less hair, even more waffle and more posh.

Then there's the dream, well it's a nightmare in truth, it's recurring always the same and I think that it's about what *really* happened.

I've been on the internet, there's a thing called Dissociative fugue or a fugue state it follows severe psychosocial stress and basically the mind runs away from events and creates an alternative, it can last days or months.

Whatever the truth is, something happened to me in that lab and I don't think that I was the only one.

The dream begins with me waking up, I'm cold and naked and its dark.

I'm lying on metal and there's metal all around me, like I'm in a box or a coffin. As I move the container shifts with me, then as my eyes adjust to the darkness I realise that there's a strip of darkness above my head that isn't so dark.

I reach into it with my fingers, it's an opening in the metal an inch wide, I push with my fingers and the metal box around me moves with me, expanding the gap another inch.

It strikes me suddenly that I'm lying in some kind of large drawer. I reach out with both hands and feel more metal under my palms and I push against it. The draw slides forward far enough for me to be able to sit up.

It's a mortuary, but it's a mortuary out of Hammer Horror or Resident evil. Three aluminium tables covered in blood and organs, blood and broken glass all over the floor, moonlight streaming through the windows and just the most dreadful smell. Everything is fresh, like it happened an hour ago. The smell is blood, there's just so much blood everywhere.

I clamber out of the drawer, watching where I put my feet, I stare around the room.

It's a mess, the smell is just so awful. There's a heap of clothes strewn across the floor, I recognise a T shirt and jeans, I pull them on shaking and trembling, then my trainers. There's clothes and underwear left, men and women's, I turn reaching for a light switch but it doesn't work there's no power.

Who would leave a lab like this? The mess, the smell I

stagger out into a corridor, I've got to find somebody.

Then there's a sound ahead of me, it sounds like a child sobbing, I hurry towards it. More broken glass cracking and chinking beneath my trainers. Then there's something ahead of me, large, standing on two legs, like a man but it isn't, it isn't human. It staggers towards me its arms open wide, it is red all over, its skin is shiny and the smell is appalling. The scarlet man, except it isn't a man how could it be? I always wake up lashing out against it, never good with super strength.

I don't know what happened to me but I do know that Adam's story isn't the truth or at the very least it isn't the whole truth.

I know there were others with me and I know that there was some kind of monster.

I don't think I was a product of the care system and I'm sure I was close to someone but if that is true, how is it that nobody has looked or is looking for me?

I've been through just about every missing person site that there is and there's hundreds of them, national and international. My accent is the same as people locally, I feel that I know the area but that's it, that's me, you now know as much as I do.

I chuck the last of the chips to a seagull who's up late and probably lost, then head for home.

For now my life is full of questions rather than answers and I know that they're going to take time to answer.

William Hendrick finished his education at Eton and boy
does it show.
In a nutshell he's posh with a capital P.
This is actually hysterical as he's set up shop in just about
the roughest most impoverished part of the capital.
I didn't take to him at first, true he offered me a job without
references but it was pretty much freelancing on a poor
wage.
I soon discovered however that all was not as it seemed,
William Hendrick ruthless businessman and entrepreneur is
far more than that, indeed he isn't really that at all.

My first job was to sort out the network in a Primary school
for special needs, one of the little dears had tipped a bottle of
coke into the back of one of the computers. The whole
system had just been donated so this wasn't ideal. Helen had
gone in to sort out the hardware in the morning, I went in
the afternoon just to get everything back up and running.
Wil came in at five to see how I'd got on, within four
minutes he's on his knees with the kids like they're his own
and when the supervisor hands him the cheque he doesn't
take it.
Hard-nosed business man eh?

As soon as he sees what I've done (and it was only basic stuff) he offers me a proper contract and a fair wage, I've worked for him ever since and believe me it has its perks.

First one is the humour.

Every visitor that comes into the office from the 'well to do' to the 'down and outs' (most are generally closer to the latter) are greeted by Wil swinging his swivel deluxe in their direction, opening his arms wide and booming 'Welcome my fine fellow, or dear lady (delete as appropriate.) Their faces are always a picture!
In this part of London Wil does not exactly fit in.

The second one is more practical.

I'm now Wil's chief programmer, or programmmer if you look at my business card (Harry the printer is on the floor above us, he's cheap but he loves a bottle or two of red.)
Now you remember what I said before about one man fighting the system and making a difference, well it turns out that you don't just need super strength and a costume.
Access to computers and a working understanding of code can be just as handy.
Wil for example had done some work for a local charity, they basically provide temporary accommodation for people

fleeing abusive relationships and then they help them to start again.

Wil realised that the reason their system had crashed was because somebody had hacked into it in a failed attempt to access their database. Wil passed the information on to the police and by doing so ruffled a few feathers.

He was informed by email in no uncertain terms that if he testified in court he'd be, and I quote, 'sorted once and for all!!'

Yep two exclamation marks! Wil however still tells anyone who'll listen, that he went ahead and nothing happened.

What Wil doesn't know is that I followed him home every night for a month and intercepted no fewer than five of the local banditry who were either waiting for him or trying to sneak up on him, two of them with blades.

All of these are still in hospital and hopefully all considering a career change for when they eventually get out.

The point is nowadays people are connected like they've never been in the past and there are always those that seek to take advantage of this.

Crime is organised and connected like never before and for those with the right skill set and motivation this presents a whole series of opportunities to drag it to its knees. Add into this that anybody who comes after me is going to have to deal with my tastefully costumed alter ego and I think you'll agree, I've found my place.

Wil sends me (as I knew he would) to the Citizens advice centre, a voluntary organisation that does impressive and important work. They're next door to the local Shopmobilty centre which also has a superb group of really likeable volunteers (not sure about their coordinator though.)

Now nearly all of these groups, charities and voluntary organisations use the same software and are all pretty much connected.

Janie runs the Citizens centre, she's Scottish, don't you forget it, and volatile. She's been married five times (three of them died) and she's now living with a fella from Doncaster. Janie always and I do mean always, wears tartan. It might be a scarf or socks, a jumper or a skirt but Janie is and always will be a Scotswoman abroad.
The truth of it is she doesn't need the tartan, her lineage is instantly apparent the second she opens her mouth. She has a gloriously thick and heavy accent which is undeniably Glaswegian and she'll go out of her way to help anybody just don't get on the wrong side of her.

Janie started to notice something odd, people were coming

in from the same area with the same problem and certain names kept cropping up in relation to a local money lender. Every time Janie checked the database there was nothing there even though she was positive that they'd been mentioned in the past. So Janie talked to Wil and Wil sent me.

'There's something in there isn't there?' She'd says from behind my left shoulder, third cigarette of the morning in her mouth.'
'I thought you were going to give them up babe,' I can call her babe, I've worked for her before.
'On my list,' she snaps, 'there's something in there isn't there?' She isn't going to go away and she isn't going to stop.'
'Yes love.'
'I knew it!' She stamps her foot on the ground and punches the side of the desk making the monitor wobble. 'I bloody knew it.'
'See there?' I point to a line of code on the screen.'
'It's all one's and noughts darling.'
'Well those one's and noughts are a Trojan horse.'
'What like classical studies?' She stubs out the cigarette in an ashtray and peers at the screen like she's looking for a horse.
'The Greek soldiers hid inside, the Trojans wheeled it into their city then when no one was looking out they came.'

'So?'

'So somebody here has clicked on something, probably something on an email, certainly innocuous but by doing so they've allowed that code to access your system then because your database is pretty basic . . .'

She throws up her hands and opens her mouth to explain.

'I know babe,' I stop her. 'Council cut backs, you haven't got the money for anything, it's a miracle you've kept this place open believe me I'm not blaming you.'

She gives me her best smile, strokes my cheek then lights up another cigarette.

'Now that code is monitoring your system, it's looking for certain names and when it finds them it deletes any mention of them.'

'The evil . . .'

'No its beautiful,' I tell her and I'm sincere.

'How can you say that?'

'Because it is,' I answer, 'Janie this code is excellent, genius even, the trick is to keep it simple and whoever has done this has done it brilliantly.'

She raises her hand and opens her mouth.

I get there first. 'Babe the code is gorgeous but what they're doing with it is foul.'

'Then we take it to the police.'

'There's no way to trace it back, the IP address will be a pay as you go SIM, soon as anyone starts looking for it it'll be long gone.'

'So there's nothing . . .' She stops seeing me smile. 'The list of names.'

'Clever girl.'

'You can get the names that it's looking for.'

'I can get the names that it's looking for.' I tell her quietly, 'but there will be consequences.'

'You're going to get *him* involved again aren't you?'

Okay I need to elaborate here a bit don't I? Long story short, this guy had been beating up his wife and knew how to work the system. The wife wouldn't make a complaint and social services couldn't find the evidence to initiate any action themselves.

A neighbour of the woman saw the man marching home from the pub clearly drunk and furious about something, the police didn't have any officers available so she rang Janie, I was working beside her when the neighbour rang and I heard everything.

Janie was going to drive to the woman's house but I stopped her, I told her I knew somebody who could sort it but I needed an address.

Janie trusted me, so she told me and I shot out to ring the 'guy' and she (I found out later) jumped into a taxi.'

By the time I'd got to the house he'd already started on her, I knew it was going to be grim but I wasn't prepared for what

I found.

The woman is five foot nothing and six stone, the guy is six four, three times her weight and he's taken a hammer from the toolbox.

That was the one and only time that I lost it and I just can't do that. It was the wife who stopped me in the end, she's covered in blood herself and she's grabbing my arms and begging me to stop hitting him.

Afterwards I very nearly gave it all up, usually I can keep my wits about me and pull my punches but that time . . .'

'Janie I explained.'

'That doesn't make it right though does it?'

'He's only human love.'

'That's not what the papers say.'

I sigh, not looking away from her stare, 'and the papers are always right aren't they?'

'Seriously Stephen,' she grabs my hand, 'what do you know about him?'

I sigh again shaking my head, 'I know he's on our side.'

'I saw him Stephen, and I saw what he did, that mask he wears, why would anybody . . .'

'You saw what he did to the guy and you saw what the guy did to his missus, you saw the size difference between them. I agree he went over the top but it's not hard to see why.'

'That doesn't make it right.'

'Nobody is saying that it was right, least of all him, I saw him afterwards there was no triumph, he was angry with himself.'

'Angry with himself?!'

She's still not having it. 'The papers say he's filled up half of the local hospitals.'

'Janie when the Jamb brothers got taken off the streets and dumped in ICU, what was your reaction?'

'Applause and I danced around the office and no I don't deny it.'

'Because they were Carson's lead boys, those two thugs hurt who they wanted to, when they wanted to with almost total impunity and those were your words.' I remind her.

'Now they *did* deserve it!'

'And that bent lawyer, look how much harm he did?'

'Agreed but there's a way to do things.'

I allow my mouth to fall open and I gape at her for a second. 'This scheme is your life Janie, why is it so important, tell me again?'

'Because the things that should work don't.' She admits quietly.

'When the things that should work disappear, when all of the safeguards are gone, then you get a vacuum and nature abhors a vacuum Janie.'

She sighs, gripping both of my hands, 'but what do you

know about him Stephen?'

I leave Janie an hour afterwards, I've already dumped the list on a memory stick and left three pages of written notes for the police's IT guy who's due down later.

I spend the afternoon removing malware from a DIY warehouse called Alf's. I'm not going to convince Janie that 'the masked dude' is with the angels, not unless I make some changes to my alter ego's appearance and that is *not* going to happen.

I should perhaps mention the mask at this point. Adam was obviously into comics and he was anxious that the costume and I quote, should engender fear in those of the underworld. The result was an expensive Halloween mask featuring a stylised skull, we wrapped some bandages around the back of it. Then Adam sourced some upholstery paint which was (roughly) the same shade of green as on the leathers.
Bizarrely Adam was right, stepping out of the shadows looking like the green death is far more effective than you might suppose, especially when you've started to build something of a reputation. The criminal classes it seems are more than just a little superstitious.

I sort out Alf's computer and head back to the flat, I'm not sure why I've got a car I seem to spend all of my time on foot, as everything's all fairly close.

Outside the flats, a 1920's obelisk called Greytowers by the residents and creepy crags by the locals, I see a police car waiting.
What if they're waiting for me? I think to myself with a smirk.

They're waiting for me.

I'm invited for a chat down at the station so I climb into the back of their car. The two coppers Ted and Angie are nice enough but they're just delivering.
They take me back to police HQ and lead me to a cramped corner office on the second floor. The room smells of sweat and bleach.
To my surprise I get a DS and a DI all to myself, Darren James and Jackie Hooper respectively.
DS Darren points me to an empty chair on the other side of the desk.
'You're probably wondering why you're here,' DI Jackie Hooper, a little too tall and painfully thin, says with something like a sneer.

'Nope I know why I'm here,' I reply, aiming for affable.

'So you admit it?' She snaps, leaning forward, with a really cold smile.

'Admit what?' I reply, genuinely confused.

'You just said that you knew why you were here,' she reminds me but I hadn't forgotten.

'That's what I said,' I agree, 'I naturally assumed that you wanted information on the Trojan horse.'

She looks back genuinely flabbergasted, 'what are you talking about?' She turns to her colleague pulling a face then back to me. 'You found a horse?' I'm not sure if it's a conscious sneer or just her face.

'A Trojan horse yes,' I say the words more slowly.

'What running along the street?' She holds up both of her hands, like I'm the one who's mad.

I sigh and lean forward, 'I am a computer programmer who this morning discovered a Trojan horse in the code of the computer at the Citizens centre, I told Janie who runs the place to contact the police. Naturally then when I'm invited in by the police for a chat I assume that . . .'

'Do we look like we're IT? DS Darren barks.

'I don't know what do police IT look like?'

'Are you trying to be funny son?' He's not happy, they were never like this on *The Bill*.

'Darren how am I . . ?'

'That's DS James to you boy.'

'Well DS James,' I snap, getting hot under the collar myself. 'I am not trying to be funny neither do I have the faintest idea of what police IT look like. Presumably they are plain clothed . . .'

'We are *not* police IT neither do either of us look anything like them!'

DS James punctuates his sentence by punching his desk and upturning a paper cup half full of cold coffee all over the open file in front of him.

With extreme self-control I stop myself from saying that neither of you look anything like Detectives either. Instead I go for a much more mundane, 'if this isn't about the computer then why am I here?'

'You are here to answer our questions and you will do so in plain English without computer speak.' DI Jackie Hooper now, it's like they're doing good cop bad cop but they've both picked the same one.

'No worries,' I try for affable again. 'But technically Trojan horse was proper plain English before it was computer speak.' See, I can't help myself.

'What are you . .?' DS Darren is properly red in the face now and has clearly long ago lost his sense of humour.

'What in the blazes are you talking about now?' He barks, or words to that effect.

'A Trojan horse is one thing dressed up as another isn't it?' They both look at me with blank expressions. 'From the

Trojan war, the Greeks got into Troy by . . .'

'For heavens sake!' DS Darren punches his desk again, causing the cup to bounce up the right way. 'You will just answer the questions, do you understand?'

I nod.

'We want to know about the conversation that you had with Mrs Stafford.' DI Jackie now, it's like tennis.

I'm genuinely blank for a moment until I realise she means Janie. 'Right, she wanted to know if anybody had got into the system, that is the program, I said . . .'

'Don't get cute with me boy,' she's right in my face, no warning, whatever happened to personal boundaries?

'What now?' I lean back away from her, 'guys I'm not telepathic, you asked me about what the two of us were talking about . . .'

'The Vigilante, the costumed guy,' she spits. 'You know full well what I mean?'

'Oh right, Any-Man why didn't you just say?' I answer calm as you like, suddenly grasping there interest.

'You know him, you're able to contact him!' She's like a lawyer in one of those courtroom dramas who's just played her ace.

'Know him no, contact him yes,' I pull my wallet from a back pocket and leaf through some business cards tucked into the back of it.

'He came into the office real late one night; he kept his mask

36

on and asked me to look at his tablet. It was locked up he wanted to know if it was just one of those things or if it was malicious, that is somebody trying to hack in.' I hand DS Darren the business card, it's blank on both sides with just a phone number scribbled in biro.

Suddenly it's all go and it's like I'm no longer there, half a dozen people are in the office, they're plugging what looks like an old fashioned phone into the phone line.
There's a senior officer too and this guy is something all together different.

Remember how I said I'm new to everything? Well it allows you to see stuff, take DS James and DI Hooper for example, I can see that they have been doing their job for too long and they've forgotten all that's important.
They're not looking at me, they're not looking to see who I am, they're just looking to see whether or not I'm lying.
They've lost sight of the fact that their job is about people first and foremost, you nail that and everything else will come with it.
You lose sight of that, you reduce people to us and them then you may as well go home.

This new guy merely glances in my direction but he's reading me like a book.

'Right!' DS James announces smugly silencing the room by holding up the business card. 'Let's have a little word with super freak shall we?' He starts stamping out the number onto the key pad.

'Um . . . I should point out . . .' I start.

'You!' DI Hooper scolds, 'be quiet.'

'It's important!' I persist undaunted.

'One more word from you . . .' She turns to the senior officer who's opened his mouth to speak. 'I'm sorry Sir but the gentleman thinks he's a comedian.'

I shake my head as the continuous ringing sound that buzzes abruptly from the speaker stops abruptly and is replaced by a dialling tone.

'He hung up without answering,' DS James blusters. 'I don't get it.'

'Mr Bishop?' The senior cop says wearily.

It takes me a second to remember that that is me. 'That's what I was trying to tell you.' I say quietly, 'he told me if I ring his number it's got to be with my phone. I didn't understand why at the time but he's obviously got a load of cheap pay as you go mobiles, if he doesn't recognise the number he obviously bins the phone.'

A lot of shouting and cursing in the room.

'I did try to tell you . . .'

'You've done nothing but give us the run around all afternoon,' James barks turning scarlet.

I however am now emboldened by the expression on the senior officers face as he looks at his DS and DI.

'I told them I found a Trojan horse in the Citizen's computer system,' I tell him aiming for affable but ruffled, 'they thought I was talking about a horse on the street.'

'We're coppers son, proper coppers, we're not computer geeks.' DS James effortlessly hammers another nail in his own coffin as the senior officer winces in embarrassment. There's a long awkward silence in the room.

'Why did he give you his card?' The senior officer turns his gaze to me, I feel like he's got X-ray vision.

'He knew I did a lot of work in the centre, he knew I'd come across a lot of things where the system was failing, where law and order weren't working as they're supposed to.' I answer calmly, not ducking his gaze.

'Then you ring us!' DS James barks from across the room.

'But the neighbour did that didn't she?' I answer calmly, she rang you because her neighbour's life was in danger. You'd had so many false alarms that you ignored it, he didn't.'

'He nearly killed the guy!'

'Yep he nearly did but the guy *would* have killed his wife this time, eighteen stone and with a hammer!'

'You seem to know all about it.'

'Janie told me all about it, she took a taxi over there as soon as it kicked off, seems like everybody was there except you lot.' I'm my own worst enemy at times; I say it before I can stop myself but the cop doesn't even blink.

'Look I'm sorry but I was *genuinely* concerned for the woman's safety, you didn't see the state Janie was in.'

'That's still aiding and abetting,' DI Hooper with another sneer, 'we can still . . .'

'Take me to court?' I'm not having it now. 'That'll look good in the press won't it? Police ignore a triple nine and then book the people who . . .'

'He's out of intensive care.' The senior cop is ignoring his officers but he hasn't looked away from me.

'Is he . . ?' I battle for a neutral expression.

'He's alive and we can and *will* charge him this time, he'll need physiotherapy and probably counselling but he'll mend in time.'

I can't quite keep the relief out of my expression and both of us know it.

'And how's his wife?' I ask firmly.

'It seems that the damage he did to her lower spine is more extensive than was initially first thought.' He answers his own expression unchanging and inscrutable.

'Meaning?'

'Meaning she'll be in a wheelchair from now on.'

I nod slowly, 'I'd like to go home now, if I may or will you be charging me?'

'You'll be going home only when we . . .'

Both myself and the senior officer ignore DI Hooper, neither of either of us even look in her direction.

'Mr Bishop if you meet that man again I would really like to hear about it, do you understand?'

I nod, my expression is back to affable.

'Furthermore if I discover that you have met him again and I don't get to hear about I will consider that as highly suspicious, do I make myself clear.'

'You do,' I answer, 'but you haven't introduced yourself.'

'I am Detective Chief Superintendant Tony Armstrong and here's *my* card.' He hands it to me. 'I'd go now if I were you.'

I pop his card into my wallet. 'Any chance of a lift back?'

'Don't push your luck.'

Fire fight – Chapter three

So the next day is really uneventful, I'm installing a database at Pearl E White's dentist (I'm really not making this up) and I've got the place to myself, there's nobody there but me and I'm to drop the keys back through the letterbox once I'm done.

Now this place like our office is still in the poorer part of London but it's North London rather than South East so I've got the car (red Fiesta 1.4 diesel, don't tell me I stint on information) parked outside.

I've barely started when I hear a gun shot. Now I guess if you live in the country the distant sound of a twelve bore might be common but out here it only means one thing.

I'm outside and in the boot of the car in seconds, I've got the jacket gloves and mask in the boot, no boots or leggings but the trousers I'm wearing are black and the shoes will do.

Another gunshot, a couple of hundred yards to my right, what people that are around are looking in that direction. I look for CCTV cameras, there's one across the square pointing the other way.

I lock the dentist and drop the keys in my pocket, then I hurry to a lane across the square.

The lane is deserted which means I can run properly, the lane leads to the High street, which I picture as I run, concentrating on the shops and businesses in the direction of the sound. There was a bank or building society on the corner.

I've got everything on bar the mask as I skid to a halt at the end of the lane and peer quickly around the side of the building.

Yep it's the building society, there's a white van on the double yellows outside, the masked driver's revving the engine like it's a formula one.

A second masked guy brandishing a sawn-off fires it into the air, causing the already screaming and running pedestrians around him to get further away.

When I first started all of this a few months back, there had been a hold-up at a bank half a mile from the office. I only found out about it afterwards, thing is a young woman was killed, the daughter of a judge no less.

They burst into the bank telling everyone to run and she froze so one of the clowns shot her and they weren't caught afterwards.

Most of the time with me it's casual violence, if there's a weapon it's usually something blunt and heavy or a blade, guns are thankfully rare but not today.

There's a dozen overflowing dustbins waiting for the council just inside the lane. They're all the old fashioned metal type with solid round lids, I pull the mask on and grab the lid of the nearest as I dash out of the lane.

I'm across the road from the building society as the idiot with the sawn-off pops two more cartridges into the breach. I can see instantly that I've got a clear shot so I take it instantly, as I run towards them I hurl the bin lid like a Frisbee at the muppet.

I aim for his stomach (there's plenty to aim for) but it slams into his chin with an almighty crack and he drops like a sack of potatoes. I shoulder charge the van, slamming into the outside of the driver's door. The door crumples around me as the force of my impact catapults the driver out of the passenger door where he face plants the pavement and the van's engine stalls.

Then I jump through the window of the bank, now in hindsight this probably wasn't the smartest thing I've ever done. In my defence I needed to get in there quickly and come on when did you ever see a superhero in a comic go in through the door?

Can I also add, for the benefit of any younger readers, that jumping through glass windows is dumb, it's also painful (more about this later.)

I'm now inside the bank, with three shotgun toting nutters one of whom has a cashier by her ponytail. The three of them are all shouting at once and all shoot at me.

I leap at the first and slap him hard, now I know a slap might seem a tad effeminate but actually for me it's quite the opposite. An open handed slap to a certain part of the head (no I'm not telling you which) with my strength will render the receiver of said slap unconscious. Remember that grip Spock had when people would just pass out when he grabbed their shoulder? Well this is my Vulcan death (unconscious) grip.

Another sawn off toting sack of potatoes crashes to the floor dropping his shotgun which lands on its handle causing the gun to fire straight up into the ceiling where a fluorescent light tube explodes and all the sprinklers come on at once. I leap for the next guy and have to use a backhanded slap this time. This does the job but although effective I don't look as cool as Spider-Man and I'm not sure that the Slapper would be an effective fear engendering name for an alter ego.

Now it's just the last guy but now I've got a problem, he's got the cashier on her knees in front of him and he's pointing the shotgun at her. He opens his mouth to no doubt yell something but I never discover what as the muppet has made the mistake of seriously underestimating a London girl. She's on her knees, her ponytail being mercilessly pulled by the idiot that's pointing a shotgun at her and what does she do?

She grabs a handful of the guy between his legs and

squeezes for all she's worth.

The guy howls like an animal then sobs like a twelve year old girl as he crumples to his knees. I step forward and punch him as hard as I dare in the middle of his face. He crumples to the floor dropping his shotgun which fires into a computer server which promptly bursts into flames despite the sprinkler's deluge.

To be honest it was a mercy, she was doing him far more damage than I did.

'You've got some guts lady,' I tell her genuinely impressed as I help her to her feet.

'That was awesome,' she declares, looking around, her glasses completely steamed up. 'Should that be doing that?' She points to the server which, as well as being on fire, is buzzing alarmingly.

'No babe, y'see the sprinklers are bunging out water but that's an electrical fire.' I tell her watching the wall go up.

'You're bleeding,' she gasps, looking down at my arm. 'They shot you!'

I look down at the expanding pool of scarlet being diluted at my feet. 'It's only a flesh wound,' I tell her trying for nonchalance.

It's not, I've got a proper gash on my forearm courtesy of jumping through a plate glass window.

'You better let me take a look at that for you,' she tells me, adjusting her glasses with a gorgeous smile. 'There's a first-

aid kit in the staffroom behind the counter, you'll have to take you're shirt off but I'll let you keep your mask on.'
And see, she really is lovely, I'm not exaggerating, she's smart, she's brave. . .
I stare at her for a moment, frantically trying to think of a witty answer, or any answer to be honest.
Suddenly there are sirens outside and cars skidding to a halt on the pavement.
'Damn,' I say loudly glancing in their direction, part of me is thankful for the distraction, the other part isn't.
I look around quickly, 'is there a back way out of here?'
'You've done nothing wrong, you're a hero,' she tells me placing her hand on my chest.
'Yeah the boys in blue aren't exactly getting that.'
'Through the staffroom, there's a door to the courtyard out the back.' She tells me, 'I could come with you if you like, sort that arm out.'
'You're really kind but . . .'

ARMED POLICE

They've got a megaphone outside.

You are surrounded, send out the hostages.

The left hand side of the building is still getting deluged by the sprinkler and the floor's like a paddling pool. The sprinkler on the right hand side stopped after a minute or so and this is now in flames.

This whole side of the building society is properly on fire now, the whole of the back wall has gone up and the ceiling tiles are melting and dribbling down like wax.

'What's your name?' I ask her, moving to drag the unconscious bodies to the door.

'Jeanette,' she answers breathlessly, wiping her glasses with a torn sleeve.

'Jeanette it has been a joy to meet you,' I tell her slinging the last unconscious muppet onto the pile.

The broken window is drawing all the smoke from the fire, leaving those outside blind to what's happening inside.

'There's only one hostage,' I shout, 'a cashier she's coming out now.'

She gives me a sad smile and a little wave then heads to the door.

'Hold your hands up and move slowly,' I advise as she goes through the door.

ON YOUR KNEES, Hands above your head

'&*%@# off, there's broken glass all over the pavement moron I'm not kneeling on that!'

I smirk and head for the back room as the ceiling collapses. I grab the first-aid kit from the wall of the staffroom and head out into the courtyard where it's a quick scramble to the roof of an adjoining building.

This has an enormous Victorian chimney, with more than enough room for a hiding superhero to crouch down out of sight whilst he attempts to patch himself up.

I can still hear Jeanette giving the police what for down on the pavement below, soon there are ambulances for the handcuffed muppets and three fire engines for the building society and a tow truck for the gangs van.

I meanwhile, am getting nowhere fast. Sticking plasters bandages, the lot, I've tried them and nothing's working. I've got a little red pool on the slates under my feet and the blood just keeps coming.

Now I'm not medical but I know it needs stitches or maybe superglue, I saw in a quiz that it was developed as a fast fix during the Vietnam war. At least that was how they answered the question but I'd changed channel before I heard whether or not the answer was correct.

I have however (surprisingly) given this situation some thought and I think I have a solution.

I leave the chimneys, I don't have an option now cos the

whole blocks gone up, there's four fire engines now. I wrap my T shirt over the wound and bandage over it. That will hold it for a while, I reverse the jacket and zip it up, mask and gloves in pockets then under cover of the smoke, I'm down a drain pipe and out of there.

Quarter of a mile along the street then down the steps and onto the tube.

I have to stand cos it's full and I hope that nobody notices the occasional drop of blood that falls from my sleeve.

After three stops I've moved and I'm hanging onto the strap above my head as the train rumbles on. With my arm raised I'm no longer spotting the floor with blood but the sensation of it dribbling down my bare chest under the jacket is far from pleasant.

Five stops later, up the escalator and out onto Tudor street find the corner with Castle street and duck down the narrow lane that connects the two. God I love lanes.

There I put the jacket on the right way and add the gloves and mask, then up a fire escape to spy on the building opposite. It's just her on the desk at the front, nobody else is in there, she's clearly writing up notes.

I look up and down the street, there's a group of kids but as soon as they've passed it's clear.

I hurry across the road to the building marked Castle street Surgery and I knock on the door.

'I'm sorry we're closed,' she answers politely from inside.

'We're only open until 2PM except Tuesdays.'

'I'm injured I need help.' I answer calmly.

After a few moments the door opens around four inches, it's on a chain. She peers out, her eyebrows jump as she recognises my mask.

'I'm not here to cause trouble but I can't just walk into a hospital.' I unzip the Jacket and pull the bloodied tee shirt from my sleeve.

She opens the door in a second and I walk in.

Y'see nowadays nurse's wages aren't too bad and for many it's a career choice because of that. Mary Kay is twenty eight and although she doesn't look it, she's old school, she became a nurse because that was all she ever wanted to be. She's got long dark hair, big blue eyes you could drown in and there's just something in her voice, I can't put my finger on it but the girl is safe and strong and she reminds me of somebody.

For someone with no past, no memories, someone that somehow is a link to what you've lost is worth their weight.

I heard about her in the Citizen's shelter, nobody had a bad word to say about her. A Christian who'd go the extra mile and help anybody. I saw her talking to Janie and knew I needed to get to know her better, suddenly now I'm looking at her and my heart is pounding.

'If it's a bullet, you need a doctor,' she tells me hands on her hips. 'Take you're jacket off.'

'It's not a bullet,' I tell her peeling the other half of the bloodied tee shirt away from the wound. 'What makes you think it's a bullet?'

'The police said on the radio, you got shot when you burned down the building society.' She tells me taking my arm and peering at the wound.

'Did they not mention the armed robbers who took a cashier hostage?' I ask as she motions for me to sit on the examination couch behind me.

'And they had sawn-off twelve bores so it's cartridges not bullets.'

She wheels over a high gilt trolley laden with bottles and sprays.

'This will sting,' she tells me taking a small aerosol spray from a plain white box.

'And as for burning the . . . 'my discourse is ruined by me yelling as the spray touches my arm.

She looks up at me with some surprise, 'you're a costumed superhero you can't yell when I put a bit of disinfectant on you.'

'It was cold!' I protest.

'You wimp!' She smirks, 'Hey that makes you Super-Wimp.'

Superb, I've gone from the Slapper to Super-Wimp in the same day, all of a sudden the Vigilante doesn't sound so bad.

'Yeah, I think I prefer Any-man, besides the point I was trying to make was that the fire was started by the robbers.'

'Was this a blade?' She asks peering at the wound.

'Glass,' I tell her as she raises her eyebrows. 'I jumped through a window.' I elaborate.

'Why?' She holds up a tube of what looks like toothpaste. 'This will sting too.'

'To get in to the building society,' I keep my voice expressionless despite the fact that it really stings.

'Didn't it have a door?' She pulls on a latex glove and rubs the crème into the wound with a single finger.

I sigh loudly, 'yes it had a door but it also had three nutters with sawn-offs and a hostage . . .' I stop when I realise she was joking.

'I'm going to need to stitch this,' she tells me making her expression stern. 'Think you'll be able to manage?'

I smirk but the mask makes it sound like I've got a cold.

'Can I ask you something?'

'Of course.'

'That mask?'

'Yep.'

'Why?' She's got a syringe now.

'What's that for?' I nod at the needle.

'Look up in the sky . . .' She sings holding up the needle.

53

'Is it a bird? Is it . . ?'

'Oh here we go.'

'No it's Super-Wimp.'

'You're really funny, you know that?'

She holds up the syringe, 'would you like me to hold your hand?'

I would actually but not for the reason she thinks.

'Get on with it.'

She stabs the needle in and I don't flinch.

'So the mask?'

'Not my idea if I'm honest, it's to engender fear in the criminal classes.'

She pulls a face, 'and how's that working for you?'

I try to think of a snappy answer but all that comes out is, 'I'm trying love.'

'Georgina Maxwell,' she answers thoughtfully after a moment. 'Do you know her?'

I shake my head.

'One of Mr Carson's boys went around to see her about her outstanding interest payment of around seventeen pounds. He broke four of her fingers, that's a little over four quid a finger.' She looks up from her stitching. 'She's well into her eighties, the thug is forty five. I patched her up, sent the info to the police even though she refused to make a complaint.

They try to help but their hands are tied and they're criminally short staffed. So I'm sat there with a terrified pensioner, she's terrified because he's coming back but you know what?'

She's looking at me now and I've got no answer.

'He never came back, he never came back because the costumed guy caught up with him and beat the living daylights out of him and a load of his mates and all.'

I still can't think of an answer.

'And the sad, simple truth of it all is this, there is only one language that that kind of people understand. 'She carries on stitching. 'A lot of the doctor's do private work as well as the NHS stuff, sometimes I'll go along with them on the agency, extra couple of quid like.'

'Go on.'

'I went into Mr Carson's house once, he's really old fashioned Jimmy Carson doesn't trust computers, keeps all his information in a locked filing room, top floor, South East corner. They say every penny he's ever lent he's got a record of.'

'Any back up?'

'There's a lock up on Station street, black corrugated door, state of the art padlock.'

'You're a revelation nurse Kay.'

'I don't recall giving you my name,' I get a proper smile for the first time, blimey was it worth the wait!

'It's over the door outside,' I remind her and she laughs as she finishes the stitches.

'I should tell you to rest it but I can see enough of your eyes to know that you won't.'

'It could be helpful to me if the police continue to think that I've been shot.'

'So you're asking me to lie for you now?'

'Not lie, just don't volunteer the information.'

She gathers up the cloths and the remains of the bloodied T shirt. 'I'll drop this off at the hospital, I know the boys who burn the waste I'll drop it in with a hastily concocted cover story.' She pulls a conspiratorial sort of face.

'Thank you.'

'Now scoot,' she glances towards the door, 'I'll lock it after you've gone.' She leaves the room, I put the Jacket back on (reversed) and remove my mask and gloves putting them in the pocket as I saunter out of the door.

The problem with Jimmy Carson is that he's ninety, been in and out of nick all his life, seen and done everything, he's not going to respond to threats and I can't go and beat up a ninety year old can I?

But I do know where he lives and yes I have worked my way through most of his boys by now.

It's midnight and I've just left the dentist after working

through the evening.

Carson's got a Doberman outside his mini mansion but she's a sweetie and clearly just for show. She brings me a chewed tennis ball which I throw for her a few times.

The garden is black with shadow but I can make out a tennis court and a swimming pool.

Then I'm up the outside of the South Eastern corner of his house, the window isn't alarmed and is easily prised quietly open.

There's a steel door, which is good it'll stop the fire from spreading and the room is just like an office filing room.

I pull all of the files off the shelves and make a heap of them in the middle of the room, then I empty the drawers of cards, thousands of them. Names, addresses and amounts, I add them to the pile.

I've got a can of petrol hanging from my belt and I drench the paperwork with it then sitting on the widow I put a match to a single card, letting it get well alight before I throw it onto the pile and the lot goes up with a sound like the bark of a dog.

I drive to the lockup which is easily found and opened, I repeat the procedure inside and then head for home, it's been a busy day.

I find out later that the door on old Carson's secret room contained neither the smoke or the flames as much as I had anticipated that it would.

It took the fire brigade two hours to get control of their second inferno of the day and according to the fire brigade there was structural damage which meant Carson and his family could not return to their manse (however loudly they demanded to.) The local Authority provided temporary accommodation for the family in a hotel on the other side of town whilst the police took the opportunity to have a properly good look around Mr Carson's manor.

It turned out that Jimmy Carson wasn't quite as good at hiding stuff as he was supposed to be.

Three stolen Waterhouse paintings and a lost Degas drawing dropped him in it from a great height and three hundred thousand in used notes did nothing to simplify matters.

The following morning I'm in the local mini mart buying a couple of cheap mobiles, all with pay as you go chips. They call them dumb phones now the girl on the desk tells me, no browsing or Youtube they're just for making phone calls.

I take a detour to another surgery at Hob street, all locked up nice and secure apart from an open attic window cos nobody's going to get in through that!

I get in easily and quietly through the attic window and hurry silently down three flights of stairs.

It's an Edwardian town house that's been converted into an office and the bottom floor is a day surgery, in effect it run as a triage for the nearby County general.
I take a ring of keys off the wall and find the one that opens the nurse's room.
Mary starts here at 8.30AM but she's usually in at eight, that's in five minutes.
I open the top drawer of her desk and place a plain business card inside with a mobile number scribbled in biro on it.
Then I lock up the room and replace the keys.
I'm scrambling back out of the attic window when I hear her keys in the front door. I settle myself on the roof leaning against a chimney and give her five minutes to get in, then I ring her mobile.'
'Mary Kay.'
'Good morning.'
'Who's this?'
'Blimey, you've forgotten me already.'
'I don't recall giving you my number.'
'Hey what can I tell you, I'm a superhero right? I have ways and means that normal mortals know little of.'

'You got it off the notice board at the Citizen's centre didn't you?'

'Yep.'

'And to what end?'

'Top right-hand draw of your desk.'

'Have you been sneaking into my office?'I hear her drawer rumble open. 'How did you get in?'

'What can I tell you M, I'm a superhero right? I have ways and means that normal . . .'

'You got in through the attic window.' She sighs, 'and what I'm M now?'

'Have you got the card?'

'It's a bit scruffy love, no graphics just a scribbled number. Isn't there a superhero union or something that could print these properly for you?'

'If you come across something, or if you need help, just ring that number on your mobile.'

'Oh right I'm a spy now am I?'

'There's a lock up on Station street, black corrugated door, state of the art padlock. Now I accept you could find out about his little filing room when you're in his house but knowing about the lockup means you've either been asking questions or at the least you keep your ears open.'

'I should go to the police.'

'And how's that worked out for you up until now?'

There's a long pause, 'I'll do what I can.'

'Mary I'm not asking you to *do* anything but if something does come up and I can help, give me a bell.'

'How's your arm?'

'It stung a bit when I fell off the roof earlier but it's okay now.'

She groans and mutters something as the buzzer in her office goes.

'I've got a patient, I've got to go.'

'Take care.'

I saunter into the office and see Wil obviously waiting for a word.

'How are you Stephen?' He leans back in his swivel master, crossing his legs and wrapping both of his hands around his knee. 'How are you doing m'boy? (At a guess he's three or four years older than I am.)' He tries for a concerned but caring expression.

I drop into my seat opposite him, grinning back broadly. 'What's up Wil?'

'Stephen really?' He blusters, 'I mean seriously my friend, can a boss not enquire about the well being of a much appreciated employee, without that employee instantly assuming that something is up?'

Helen talking to a customer on headphones in the corner smirks quickly in my direction.

'Wil I haven't known you that long but it already seems that you've been in my life forever.'

'Oh my dear fellow what a lovely thing to say.'

'And because of that my friend I do indeed know when something is up.'

'Well there isn't anything really . . . important because obviously if there was we'd have sorted it out man for man as it were. However I, as your employer and I hope also, as your friend I would be sadly neglecting my duties if I didn't come straight to the point without . . . ah beating about the bush . . . um . . .'

' It's Janie isn't it?'

Wil nods frantically, relief all over his face. 'She has tried to ring you on . . . several, numerous . . .'

'And I didn't take her call, any of them.'

'Can I ask you why m'boy?'

'Because Wil she dropped me right in it with the police.'

Wil looks suitably shocked. 'Stephen m'boy if you're in any kind of trouble.'

I sigh and tell him the story, Wil listens intently and clearly fascinated.

'So he was here, Any-Man, in my office?' Wil blusters looking quickly around the room.

'Wil he sat in *your* chair'

Wil's expression is of a lottery winner who's just found out that his second ticket has come up trumps as well. 'Any-man sat in *my* chair?'

'Yep,' I lie effortlessly (although I have had a few spins in it when nobody was looking.) 'I had his tablet on my desk, he sat in your chair, he even span it right around like you do some times.

Wil's filling up now, 'he span around in my chair, just like I do?' Wil pulls an immaculate handkerchief from his suit pocket and dabs his eyes. 'Did he say anything?'

'He said this is a really cool chair.'

Wil claps his hands together an expression of sheer bliss on his face. 'Oh my dear boy why didn't you tell me?'

I let my head drop, 'well to tell you the truth Wil I was a little bit ashamed.'

'Oh my dear boy,' Wil is all instant consolation. 'Why on earth would you think . . ?'

I raise my head with a guilty expression,' I didn't charge him mate.'

Wil laughs aloud and slaps me on the shoulder, the blow would have put a lesser man on the floor.

'Of course you didn't charge him Hendrick's Computer Consultancy has always put itself at the disposal of those that have the gumption to stand up and to . . . um . . . to make a stand.' He leans forward in his chair and glances furtively around the room. 'I've seen him too,' he whispers. 'Really?' I wheel my chair closer.

'Well not so much saw him, I saw what he did.'

'You saw what he did?'

'Remember when I had those threats about testifying?'

I nod quickly.

'Well on the Wednesday night I went and stayed at my Sister's on Hamilton street, she was away and wanted someone to watch Harry.'

'The dog?'

'The parrot,' Wil whispers. 'Now it's the top end of Hamilton street. . .'

'Oh very nice,' Helen interrupts.

'With the trees along the pavement.'

'Oh I love trees in the pavement,' Helen sighs leaning back in her chair.

'Best thing about living in London,' I agree with her.

'Now y'see I just had a feeling that something wasn't right, I'm ex TA* remember.' Wil continues undaunted.

*Territorial army.

'I just kind of knew that something wasn't right.'

Helen and I nod in unison.

'Somebody's following me I thought.' Wil whispers rolling his eyes.

'What did you do?' Helen whispers.

'Well see there were plenty of people about and I soon

reached the house and went in.'

'Go on.'

'Well I put me fish and chips in the microwave then outside the kitchen window there's this dreadful scream.'

'Blimey,' Helen and I echo.

'So I went outside with the poker and guess what was stuck twenty feet up the tree at the back of the lane behind the house?'

Helen and I shake our heads.

'Harry Norbett.'

'What Carson's thug?'

'The very same, two broken arms and a broken jaw, they had to get the fire brigade to hoist him down.

'What the hell was he doing up a tree outside your Sister's house?'

'I think it was *him!*

'Any-Man you mean?' I gasp.

'Fireman I talked to said he'd been thrown into the tree, Harry Norbett is nineteen stone if he's a pound, who else could do that?'

'Blimey,' Helen and I mutter together.

'Don't you realise what this means?'

Helen and I shake our heads.

'He's recognised us, Any-Man, we're on his radar and he's fighting alongside us, this is our destiny my friends.' Wil nods solemnly then he turns to me. 'Stephen?'

'Yes Wil.'

'Go and see Janie.'

'I'll go and see her tomorrow Wil, you have my word.'

I work late because I have an ulterior motive, you remember I mentioned Angie one of the PCSO's who took me to the police station?

Well after DCS Tony Armstrong threw me out, I bumped into her in the lift and she offered me a lift home. She just had to do one thing first and that was to drop off a file in the computers section on the top floor.

Now I obviously, waited respectfully by the lift as she went but naturally it gave me chance to have a quick look around.

Standard locks on the windows, no motion sensor alarms, a single server at the back of the room, all desk tops and laptops no doubt networked to it and no CCTV.

Thing is, its minimum security, it's a room at the very top of the building in the middle of town who's going to be daft enough to try and break in.

I watch a spotty lad in shirt sleeves drop into his chair and switch on his computer, whilst he waits for it to warm up he opens his unlocked right-hand top desk draw and he pulls out a notebook.

I smile to myself as he types in his password, he probably

goes around schools lecturing the local kids on computer security and then he keeps all his own passwords in a book in his drawer.

Typical programmer.

Angie returns with a smile and we take the lift down to the garage beneath the building.

A couple of days later I'm on the police HQ roof at midnight, the windows are harder than I first thought but there's several skylights on the roof also.
The moon slides out from under a cloud and bathes the rooftop in pale blue light. The reflection of my skull mask abruptly appearing on the glass skylight startles me for a second. It happens often, you forget that you're wearing the mask until you suddenly catch sight of your reflection.
I ease the skylight open and drop silently onto the thin carpet.
I have to admit it just feels wrong, the office is in darkness, just tiny blue and red lights glowing on hardware.
I hurry to the desk of the lad I saw before and within moments I've used his notebook to access the system and switch it to safe mode. From here I can access the code and in no time I've networked another computer to the system. It

won't show of course, it's on a list of computers that had been networked previously but have since been removed, just a list of numbers that don't matter anymore.

Then I use a memory stick to get *my* Trojan horse into their system.

It's the same code that I've modified, it's not going to do any harm but it will let me know what they're up to and if anybody else is hacking into their system.

Finally I access the logs and remove all the records pertaining to what I've just been doing.

I'm out of there in less than an hour.

The following morning I'm in the citizen's shelter and working my way through the name list. There's many that I don't know and this makes sense. It would be foolish to believe that Carson was the only crime boss but if all these names are dodgy then blimey have I got some work to do.

Fiona one of Janie's volunteers is running the shop as it was Celtic V Rangers last night so Janie will be late and no doubt hung over.

I've tightened up her security to such an extent that it'll take a Challenger tank to access her database now and by the time she rolls in, I've got all that I needed.

'Fiona, coffee babe, she exclaims falling through the door.
'Stephen what a lovely surprise,' she manages clearly surprised to see me. 'I've been trying to get in touch.'
'Yeah sorry about that,' I reply without humour. 'I've been helping the police with their enquires.'
 Her face falls, 'look Stephen . . . I . . .'
'Why didn't you tell me Janie?' I ask her pointedly. 'I've bent over backwards sorting things out here for you.'
'Look love, I couldn't look the other way, the man nearly died . . .'
'No he didn't! ' I answer her, folding my arms across my chest. 'He's already out of intensive care and they expect a full recovery.'
'Oh well that's good to hear,' she stammers. 'At least that . . .'
'Not so good for his missus though Janie.'
Janie's face falls.
'Seems the damage that he did to her spine was worse than they originally thought.'
'That doesn't make it right.' She whispers.
'Well it doesn't matter now, I can't ring him anymore the police made sure of that.'
'It's probably for the best.'
'Yeah,' I answer sullenly, looking her in the eye as she looks away. 'Let's just hope you don't get anymore wife beaters eh?'
'Stephen it's not as simple as . . .'

'Your system is back up and running and it's secure.' I tell her flatly as I leave.

I hadn't meant to be so blunt; it just came out that way. I sit on the wall outside the chippie with a beef burger in batter and chips.
How do you make this work?

As I've said before it's not the police's fault, sure there are one or two bad apples that think that they're God's gift but the bulk of them are trying to do an impossible job with a fraction of the manpower that they need.
And Janie's right, I over reacted to the wife beater but the other side of that argument is that if I hadn't reacted at all he'd have killed her. I saw him and he'd lost it before I did. What are you supposed to do, when the only way to stand up for law and order is to break the law?

Janie would have been a good contact but only if she trusts me which she clearly doesn't.
I can spy on her now just like I can spy on the police and of course it's illegal but my motivation is not and has never been, personal gain. I'm not interested in snooping on anybody's personal affairs but I am interested in those that know how to work the system. Those with clever and expensive lawyers who are at their beck and call.

As I've mentioned before, it's like I'm seeing it all for the first time, I can see how things are and why they're failing and it always boils down to money, to resources.

I cannot understand why people put up with it and tolerate it, maybe I just need to visit Downing street and bounce the millionaire politicians around the cabinet office for a few minutes.

I finish the beef burger and throw the last of the chips to a handful of seagulls.

There's a lawyer, Emma by name, she helps out at the citizen's centre. A formidable woman who doesn't suffer fools. Out of the blue I decide to have a chat with her, I pull my smart phone from my pocket and pop into the citizen centres volunteer database to get her address.

'Are you seeking my blessing?'
 Fair play this is one strong woman, I turn up on the veranda of her fourteenth floor suite and knock on her window like a nervous boy scout. She doesn't bat an eye, just points me to the door which she unlocks with some effort.
'Is that why you're here, you should know I'm retired.'
'You'll never retire Emma.' I answer easily.

'That mask is repulsive, can't you take it off?'

'The fewer people who know who I am the safer everybody is.'

'That's rather dramatic but then, she pauses reaching for a kettle, the fires at Mr Carson's properties, that was you I assume?'

I nod.

'You're clearly not worried about making enemies.'

'What's the alternative? The police have known about Carson for years.'

She nods. 'I concede that there is all too clearly a vacuum and you have the wherewithal to fill it but the law exists for a reason but the moment that you start to break one law in order to satisfy another it becomes an extremely slippery slope. Tea of Coffee?'

'I'm fine,' I tell her shaking my head. In your career you've surely seen instances of the law failing and not working as intended.

'Of course,' she pours boiling water onto a tea strainer, I've not seen one for years, at least I don't think I have. 'But I didn't go after them and beat them up.'

She carries her tea in a china cup to the settee and motions for me to sit in the armchair opposite her.

'But!' she points a fat finger at me, 'I didn't chase after anyone and beat them up because I couldn't, I was simply not in a position to do that.'

'Oh I don't know,' I chuckle back, 'you don't strike me as a shrinking violet.'

She grabs both of her ample bosoms and presses them together. 'You think I could lever these into a skin tight leather cat suit boyo?'

I laugh aloud, any doubts I've had about coming have evaporated now.

'Very many years ago, a junior partner in the law firm I was assigned to, tried it on with me at the Christmas party, when I refused he punched me in the mouth and then dared me to tell anyone.'

She holds up a hand seeing me clench my fist. 'He died years ago before you demand his name and race off into the night for grim revenge.'

I nod, 'go on.'

'I'd never been hit before, the pain, the embarrassment of it was extraordinary, he's there telling everyone that a champagne cork had done it and I'm stood there mopping up the blood with a table napkin and I don't say a word to contradict him.'

She takes another long sip of her tea, 'I felt so ashamed for so long and there was nowhere that I could go for justice. I was nothing and he was well on his way, nobody was going to believe me. Now if you ask me, if I'd had the power the wherewithal to go after him and give him a proper hiding would I do it?'

She takes another long sip and stares silently at the swirling surface of the tea.

'Yes, no question, I'd have punched his bloody lights out!' I smile under the mask, 'there was this guy, he was huge and he's beating his wife, she's tiny, the size of a ten year old and the guys got a hammer, I swear I don't know how I didn't kill him.'

She leans back in her seat, 'do you know that the vast majority of people don't have a clue what's going on around them. Ask most people about what they think evil is and they'll tell you about hammer horror, Frankenstein and Dracula. But the reality is there's another world, Social workers and police see it but their hands are so often tied. The lawyers and magistrates do what they can but all too often the law seems more concerned about the rights of the perpetrator than the rights of the victim.'

'People can be responsible for the greatest kindness and the most marvellous grace but people can also be ugly and do things that are very grim. Do you know the name Andrew Small? You've had dealing with him recently, you broke his jaw, scapula and collarbone with a dustbin lid.'

'He had a shotgun.'

'Oh I'm not defending him, believe me, what about Eleanor Blackmoor?'

'I know that name, she was on the news some weeks back, a judges daughter killed in a bank raid.'

She nods quickly, 'by Mr Andrew Small, he told her to move, she didn't move as quickly as he thought she should, so he shot her point blank in the face with a twelve bore. He ended all that she was, all that she could have been, the children that she might have had and the grandchildren all gone. Gone forever because of one petulant spiteful bully who thought himself entitled to just take whatever it was that he wanted.'

'You knew her, Eleanor?'

She nods, 'I taught her French and I taught her to play the piano.' She pauses studying again the surface of her tea. 'Her Father Christopher was a colleague, a very singular judge, perhaps a little too lenient, you should look up his Wikipedia page. As for you, you're nibbling around the edges; you're poking a hornet's nest with a stick.' She looks up slowly, her eye's finding mine. 'I'm not saying that you aren't effective but you are a blunt instrument and before we look at that you should be aware that you have more pressing matters.'

'Go on.'

'Nature, just as it abhors a vacuum, is also often an arms race is it not?'

I nod in agreement but I'm not sure where she's going.

'Mr Small and his associates are either now in hospital under guard or in jail, apart from Mr Steven Yardley who was the driver, now Mr Yardley is an American citizen, wanted in the States and the extradition order is already in place.'

I nod again with more interest this time.

'Normally extradition is an exceptionally tiresome drawn out procedure but in Mr Yardley's case it was organised over-night. The RAF have a Hercules that's visiting an airbase virtually next door to the relevant detention centre in the States, so so far so good.'

'There's a *but* coming isn't there?'

'The military are currently trialling a new type of steel cage for detention, flat packed, ten foot square. If you need a secure cell you can have one up in minutes anywhere you want one.'

'So Mr Yardley was in one of these . . ?' I guess.

She nods after another slurp of tea, 'locked up safe and sound in an RAF hanger in front of a CCTV camera.'

'Something happened to him?'

I watch the blood drain from her face. 'Oh yes m'boy, something happened to him alright.' She puts her cup down on the neat side table beside her chair and walks to her window, looking down at the city below with her arms folded across her chest.

'What I am about to tell you is between us?'

'You have my word.' I answer quickly.

'At three seventeen AM two nights ago, somebody dropped onto the roof of the cage, they reached down through the bars grabbing Mr Yardley by the throat with one hand. They then pulled him up and out through the bars.'

'What? How wide are the bars?'

'The gap between the bars is five inches.' She answers without looking around.

'So he bent the bars to pull him through?'

'It's a special type of hardened steel, military spec, I doubt even you could move them.' She answers quietly, 'no he pulled the man's body through a five inch gap.'

'But that . . .'

'Would have broken every bone in his body?' She interrupts, turning to face me. 'Yes, well all bar fingers and toes. The police and RAF surgeons did the post mortem together, the military doctor said that Mr Yardley's wounds were consistent with having been run over by a tank.'

'Blimey who would have the strength . . .?' A sudden thought stops me. 'It wasn't me.'

'We know,' she answers quickly. 'The CCTV was poor quality but the perpetrator was neither your age nor your build, he was described as elderly and slightly built.'

'And he lifted a guy with one hand and dragged him through a gap that small?' I splutter.

'Be careful!'

I nod slowly but my mind is racing.

'They've moved the others from the gang into secure locations.'

'You think he was after all of them?'

77

'They don't know, he's either a specialist from the States over here for Yardley or he's home grown and possibly after the whole gang. Either way you need to be careful . . .' An alarm pings on her watch, 'and you need to go, for now at least.'

'Okay . . . I . . .'

'I have three town councillors and a pizza on their way up.'

'Thanks for your time,' I turn for the balcony.

'Thursday evenings after Enders is best for me.' She shouts after me as I scramble down the side of the building.

I'm into the police computer within minutes but there's nothing. They've got details of the gang up until the time that they were taken into custody and then everything's forwarded to *'Division'*, whoever they are and whoever they are their firewall is excellent, there's no obvious way in. This is going to take time.

Mantis – Chapter five.

A week later and I've got nowhere with Division, most of the police software is surprisingly standard not so Division, I'm not sure of who they are or where they're based but there's no way that I'm going to be able to get into their system without anybody knowing that I've been there.

There's been nothing on the News or in the papers about Yardley but there has been news about something else, a costumed super villain no less but this is no frail elderly man.

The woman known as Mantis beat up seven security guards at a private Museum in Edinburgh.

The only description of the girl that the police could get from one of the battered guards was 'fit and foreign.'

There's lots of CCTV footage as well and I've got to admit she looks the part, skin tight green lycra, a yellow cycle helmet and two samurai swords. Yes you read that right and blimey she's fast.

Now see I'm wondering if this is what Emma meant by an arm's race but the thing is she's not local. One job in Edinburgh then all the rest of the sightings have been in Cardiff!

I keep telling myself that it's nothing to do with me and that I've got enough problems of my own but it's a bit of a coincidence that she's turned up at the same time as the other guy.

In the end I tell Will that I've tested positive for Covid and I'll be working from home. I then head for Paddington with my laptop, costume and a change of clothes in my rucksack. An hour and a bit later I'm walking along the station of the Welsh capital and by lunchtime I've got a room for the week in the *Travellers Rest* (think budget Motel meets Youth Hostel) the room's tiny but private and with free WiFi.

As well as the National News in the early evening I have Wales Today which gives me all the local news and gossip. More to the point it's got more information about the young lady in question.

She's been spotted several times in the last few days, always at night and always on the rooftops. The police say that she's broken into numerous locations residential and commercial but nothing has been stolen. She wallops anyone who tries to stop her and she appears to be looking for something but other than that nobody has got a clue as to her motive. The police advise anybody that sees her not to engage with her but rather to ring them at once.

See why I'm intrigued?

I spend the afternoon taking in the sites of Cardiff, the Castle is cool and Forbidden Plant is awesome (if compact) more to the point, I get a good look at the City. Loads of lanes and arcades, plenty of Victorian brick work. Finally I sit outside a burger bar eating my supper as the sun goes down.

One of the problems any potential costumed hero to be encounters nowadays is CCTV. Now don't get me wrong I know they make the streets safer and have saved countless lives but can you imagine how Clark Kent would react if he found one in his favourite phone booth?

When I'm certain I'm not being observed I put on and zip up the jacket I've been carrying then pull on my gloves and mask.
I'm sat in the shadows of an alcove at the top of a staircase in the corner of one of the roof tops pretty much in the middle of the High street. There's a full moon tonight and I've got a good view of the roofs all around.
The brunette on the news reckoned the mantis girl was out most nights, which meant that my plan was sure to work. Isn't that so often the case mind? The simple plans are so often the most effective.

I sit there all night waiting for her like a fool, there's no sign of her.

What an idiot, I've come all this way, no proper plan and spent the night playing spot the bat, what a complete pillock!

I shin down a drain pipe, remove mask and gloves (after double checking for cameras) and find a cafe in the arcade. After a full English breakfast and a coffee with extra I'm feeling so much better, the plan was fine, it's not like there were that many other options after all, just my timing was off. I'll try again tonight.

I spend the morning taking a bus trip around the bay and I'm back by late afternoon and considering my options for supper. There's Italian, do I like Italian? I had a great pizza for lunch and I know I like Chinese but that's because there's a great one across the road from my flat, sweet and sour pork you'd kill for.

My important deliberations are abruptly curtailed by the sound of several gunshots, which have everybody around me gaping up at the rooftops across the square.

I run like I'm running away but I've got my eyes on a camera on the corner, the moment I'm out of its field of view I'm checking for others, one only and facing the other way.

There's a multi-storey car park I'm in it in a second, there are cameras around the exit but they're focussed on number plates. I dash past and up the ramp, pulling my costume on as I run, there are stairs in the corner and I take them four at a time.

In one minute I'm on the roof and it's like a film set.

The roofs across the square are lower, there's a handful of guys all dressed the same, black shirts and trousers with those phones that you can wear around your ear and always look ridiculous. They've all got hand guns, three are down another three are all shooting at something or someone on the adjoining roof which I can't see because of the angle. There's a girl there also, smartly dressed blouse and skirt like a uniform, she's right on the edge of the roof.

I'm running towards them in an instant, although I honestly haven't got a clue about what's going on.

There's an adjoining rooftop that I can jump to and from there I can jump across to the building that's adjoining the one where everything is kicking off.

I race across and leap for the roof, the gunmen seeing me coming, all turn and fire in my direction.

I land and roll onto my shoulder, then leap for the nearest gunner, a well aimed slap takes him out of the picture. His two colleagues, who've just run out of bullets, both leap onto me, one pistol whips me whilst the other wraps his arm around my throat and attempts to drag me to the floor.

I respond by grabbing each by the ear and banging their heads together.

The girl meanwhile has been running towards us and seeing me she skids to a halt and puts her hand up under her skirt. Even as I'm wondering what on earth it is that she's looking for, she pulls out a gun and points it straight at me.

'Back away from them now or . . .'

She doesn't get to finish as half a house brick slams into the side of her head and sends her sprawling off the roof.

I dive after her, catching sight of her attacker as I go, bright green, skin tight, her lovely face spoilt by the look of complete hatred that she's flashing in my direction.

I catch first the girl and then the ledge of a veranda a dozen feet below.

The veranda is covered in cardboard boxes and there's an open door. I push through carrying the girl who's just moaning now.

It's a shop, it looks kind of like Olivander's in the film. Shelves and stacked up tiny boxes everywhere.

There's a guy, fifty something, sharp suit, dodgy teeth. 'Who in the blazes . . ?' He gasps as I hand him the semi conscious girl. Anybody would think that a living skeleton bursting out of his storeroom and handing him a barely conscious young woman was an unusual occurrence.

'She needs an ambulance,' I tell him urgently pushing her

into his arms, 'she's either Police,' I tell him remembering the red plastic clip over the trigger of the gun she was carrying. 'Or she's a dangerous assassin!' I add helpfully, turning back up the staircase and hurrying back the way I came.
From the veranda its back onto the roof, where there are now six unconscious dudes with matching earpieces.

Besides them stands Mantis and one glance tells me that her mood has not improved.

But first let me describe her to you, see my costume is sort of Halloween on a budget, this girl however has really made an effort.
The costume is a bright pale green and honestly it looks like it's been sprayed on, tight doesn't begin to convey it. Every muscle and every curve, I'm trying not to stare really I am but bloody hell!
This girl would stand out in any crowd in any country, her figure is stunning and her face, what I can see of it and minus the *if looks could kill* is gorgeous.
It's not like she's wearing a praying mantis costume its more that everything she wears and the way she carries it just suggests a praying mantis and one poised to rip the head off a male that's come to close.
The modified cycle helmet that protects her head is yellow her blonde hair behind it is in a bun. The two form an oval

on the top and the back of her head shaped and coloured exactly like the eyes of the real creature. The two identical silver samurai swords quivering in her hands look for all the world like the folded claws of a mantis, ready to strike. More to the point, the way she stands, the way she looks, the way she's poised, everything about her says enraged predator.

Somebody somewhere, somehow has seriously upset this woman, she is completely furious, she is utterly incensed. It doesn't escape my attention that I'm the only person who's up here with her that's conscious and it's me that she's glaring at.

'Well hi there little lady, do you need somebody to give you a hand down.' I say it without thinking and before I can stop myself, I really don't know why I do it, it's like my brain and my mouth are completely estranged.

She answers me with a scream, there's no other word for it, then she leaps forward kicking out and sending me somersaulting over backwards.

Normally punches and kicks I barely feel, not so this time. I'd forgotten what a proper kick in the ribs felt like and I don't enjoy the reminder, I fly over backwards and crash down onto the roof.

She's on me in an instant, in a blur of speed, she's got her knee in my chest pinning me to the roof, one blade against my throat the other hovering over my face.

'Pourquoi interfères-tu?' She hisses.

'I don't speak Welsh,' I stammer back. 'Do you speaksey English?'

Now in my defence most Welsh people don't speak Welsh anymore, especially in the South of the country and I'm English (I think!) I've been in the Welsh capital for two days and the only welsh language I've come across has been written on the street signs, nobody's is actually using it!

'nos da cymru,' I try cos the girl on Wales Today said it and it sounded friendly.

'Je ne suis pas gallois crétin je suis français!' She shrieks, still clearly furious.

'Wait a second, francais that's French, you're French right?' I gabble, do I speak French, I mean did I? She's still on top of me and despite the snarling and aggression (not to mention her knee in my sternum) it's all suddenly rather intimate.

'Um germ apple Any-Man.' I try for calm authority.

Her features harden into a look of complete disgust. 'De quoi tu parles au nom de Dieu?'

'Erm . . ?'

'Tu n'es pas censé être ici.'

'. . .'

'Pas étonnant que tu aies des bandages sur la tête,' she scowls, 'ont-ils enlevé votre cerveau?'

'Now going by her tone and expression I'm guessing that

that last one was an insult and I can't help but feel like I'm losing the initiative here.'

'I know about Steven Yardley,' I play my ace, my voice calm despite the steel against my throat.

How long has it been since I've been this close to a woman I wonder, she's intoxicating (if volatile) she's panting slightly and she's hot, I can feel the heat from her body, see her pulse in her throat. She smells equally of sweat and expensive perfume.

'Steven Yardley,' I repeat more slowly, annunciating carefully.'

She looks at me incredulously for a moment, 'où est le codex d'Estelle?'

'Er . . .'

'Que savez-vous du codex?'

'He was in a cage, with the RAF . . .'

'Dis moi vite.'

We're clearly at cross purposes here and more to the point here is suddenly becoming very public.

There are police siren's all around and a helicopter buzzing towards us now like a huge slow bluebottle.

I shove her to the side with both arms, a normal person would have been off the other side of the roof, she just hops to her feet like I helped her up.

'Ce n'est pas votre idiot d'affaires,' She spits pointing a

sword in my direction.

I go to grab her.

This was a mistake.

She flicks the sword tip along my arm as she dances out of the way. I feel the bite of the blade as it slices down from my shoulder to my elbow.

Simultaneously something wraps itself around both of my ankles.

I look down to see one of the guys dressed in black wrapped around my feet and hanging on for grim death.

Armed police, do not move, put your hands on your head and drop to your knees.

A voice with a thick Welsh accent booms from a megaphone under the helicopter. A door in the side of which is open and there's a guy with a baseball cap and a sniper rifle pointing in my direction.

To my right Mantis skips away over the rooftops like a ballerina leaving stage and all of a sudden nobody's interested in her anymore.

Do as I tell you, QUICKLY!

The helicopter's circling me now, the guy with the mic is on the seat beside the pilot, the guy with the gun keeps it pointed at me.

'You tell me not to move then you tell me to move my hands and get on my knees, which is it?'I shout up to them, 'I can't do one without doing the other.'
My perfectly reasonable question seems to throw the helicopter crew for a moment or two.

On your knees now!

I nod and kneel but only to be able to grab the arms of the guy who's wrapped around my feet. I pull him off and bolt forward under the helicopter, as it rises and turns to bring the gun man around to face me, I run to the edge of the roof and leap for the adjoining building.
I land, roll and then race along the roof. The helicopter comes after me and there are clearly officers on the staircases, in fact there are police everywhere. One minute there's not enough of them to manage their area then the next there's an army of them!
I race to the edge and see that the adjoining building is a lot lower. I scramble over and then down the side, I jump for this roof then race across it then drop on to the roof of a bus shelter that's parallel to it below.

The cut is bad, at least as bad as the glass from the bank and it's the same arm! More to the point I've got no friendly nurses in Wales (that I know of) but my problem at the moment is the helicopter.

'How do you hide from a helicopter?'

Well as it turns out, in Cardiff at least, that isn't as much of a problem as one might suppose.

Cardiff town centre is honeycombed with arcades, everybody is running towards the sirens to see what's going on. I just slide from the roof of the bus shelter and into the nearest empty arcade.

With my mask and gloves in my jacket the only thing that stands out now is the bloody cut along my arm. I carry my jacket over my shoulder pressing that side of my arm into my T shirt.

Now I am so glad that I checked out these arcades yesterday. I know that this particular one has six potential exits, the helicopter will have seen me enter so he's no doubt buzzing them now and calling for officers on the ground to come to the arcade.

I can't stay in here but I need them to think that I have. I look around at the shops, there's a large bookshop where a single assistant is trying to help a group of tourists.

I walk into the shop and flash her a smile, she looks stressed, the tourists are Chinese and can't understand her, they keep pointing to a map and saying 'where?'

It's obviously a day for language difficulties.

There are stairs at the back of the shop and a sign saying staff only. I slip up them silently, trying to look like I own the place whilst I drip blood on the carpet.

Nobody in the shop below notices. Upstairs there's a small kitchen, a storeroom and a toilet.

I pinch a plastic carrier bag from the storeroom and jam my jacket into it then climb up onto the draining board and stick my head out of the open window.

The helicopter is near and coming closer but I can't see it, I wait until its circled overhead then scramble silently out of the window and down into the yard below.

All the shops are linked at the back by a long covered lane where goods and stock can be delivered. I hurry along it, sticking to the shadows.

I can hear police all around, they're racing along the arcade on the other side of the wall. I reach the entrance to the lane, I can hear the helicopter but it's not overhead and there's people everywhere on the street.

The blood's just running down my arm and dripping in the carrier bag, the cut is down the back of my arm so I keep this pressed in to my side.

There's a taxi waiting for hire in a bay across the street, my heart leaps and I hurry over.

'Mate can you take me to the nearest hospital, my missus just rang, she forgot the little un's inhaler and she's having an attack so they've taken her in but I don't know the name of the hospital.'

'Hop in son,' he tells me cheerfully starting the car, 'there's two close but only one's got a casualty department.'

'That's the one!' I tell him cheerfully, scrambling in to the back. 'They told her they were taking them to casualty.'

'Won't be long mate, don't you worry!' He tells me with a flash of smile in the mirror. 'Down here from the smoke are you?'

'Aye, bit of a break you know, then she goes and forgets the inhaler.' I tut loudly, 'Women eh, can't live with them . . .'

'Can't live without them.' The driver finishes with a smirk before shouting obscenities at a Corsa that cuts him up.

For one awful moment I think that the helicopter is about to turn and follow us but thankfully it continues circling the arcade.

The hospital, as he said, isn't too far at all (although he charges me £25!)

My mind's racing trying to come up with another story when a bank of scaffolding up against a new build in the grounds of the hospital solves the problem for me.

I make a note of the name of the builders and read the sign beside it.

CEDS Community Economic Development Scheme in conjunction with the Welsh Office bring you the new Dougie Douglas CT and MRI suite. We plan to open in the first quarter of 2024.

Somebody has drawn a cartoon of a laughing face beside the 2024!

I hurry to the other end of the site and the casualty building, nobody's looking outside so I hurl the bag with my jacket up onto the roof then walk into the building holding my arm.

There's a queue outside a glass window where a woman in uniform is asking questions.
I stand there patiently holding my arm and dripping blood over the floor. A nurse who's just stepped out of a door marked *triage* sees me and hurries over.
'What on earth have you done?' She asks peering at my arm.
'Oh I'm with R G and the boys Sister,' I tell her with a smile. She looks blank.
'R G Jennings, the builder's across the site, we're building your new scanner lab.'
'Oh of course yes, sorry,' she blusters. 'Have you had an accident?'
'Bit of one yes,' I concede holding up my now scarlet arm.

'See it was Mickey's turn on the angle grinder but Mickey well see he's a good lad but he's got this bit of a nervous twitch and . . .'

'Come with me,' she flashes a scowl at everybody else in the queue then hurries back to triage rapidly followed by a woman from the reception office brandishing a clipboard and an electronic tablet.

'Barbara we haven't taken the gentleman's details.'

'Yvonne look at his arm, you can't leave him bleeding to death in a queue.'

Yvonne opens her mouth to answer but catches site of my arm and turns green instead.

'I can give you my details now if you like,' I tell Yvonne anxious to stop her and Babs coming to blows.

'Shirt off!'

'Why Barbara this is so sudden,' I quip as she sits me on the end of a long green leather couch.

'I didn't tell the gentleman to wait in the queue neither did I see him there do you really think . . .' Yvonne's still not happy.

'Yvonne calm yourself, I just came in and got into the queue cos it said queue here, I was only there a moment, no harm done,' I tell her soothingly.

'There's another cut here, recent.' Babs peers at my arm.

'And that's my point, he's a good lad but how many times are we going to turn a blind eye to . . .'

'I'm going to have to log this.' Barbara tells me with a frown pulling on a pair of plastic gloves and reaching for the antiseptic.

'That's what the tall guy said, your health and safety dude, he was lecturing Stan about the first accident when Mickey slipped the second time.'

'Health and safety, you don't mean Andrew do you? Andrew Fields.'

'Aye, That's him.' I tell her wincing at the sting of the antiseptic. 'Furious he was.'

'You said he was tall, Andrew's shorter than I am.'

'Builder's humour love, Mickey's nick-name is stable.' I answer calmly.

She starts stitching as Yvonne brandishes her tablet, 'Name.'

'Terry White, 27 Tunnel terrace, Reading.

'You're a long way from home Terry, what are you doing over here in Wales?' She asks as she types in my postcode and phone number.

'Building your CT and MRI suite.'

'Lovely and your Doctor?'

'Old Jethro, his clinics down the road from us, can't remember his surname.'

Yvonne frowns squinting at her tablet, 'well the nearest is Thompson's on Mount street but that's . . .'

'Thompson's' I exclaim, snapping the fingers of my free hand. 'That's the one.'

Terry White was a mate of Adam's, we never met but I fixed his laptop as a favour for Adam and I can still remember his details.

Barbara continues stitching whilst Yvonne scurries back to reception.

We sit in silence as Babs carefully stitches up my arm, she looks tired and she's probably not paid that well but she is so good at what she does.

'Right, that's the cut sorted but Doctor's going to want to see it, I assuming you had a tetanus jab after the last one.'

'Of course,' I tell her lying through my teeth.

'The cut wasn't that deep but it was extremely long and very neat.'

'We'd just changed the disc,' I tell her nodding with understanding. 'It were brand new, done my arm before it got anywhere near the concrete.'

'We might need to keep you in over-night just for observation and we'll need to do your bloods.'

'No worries,' I tell her affably pulling my T shirt back on. 'What do you want me to do?'

'Go back to the casualty waiting room and someone will come for you. It'll be a couple of hours I'm afraid.'

'No worries, it'll be safer than working with Mickey, is there a toilet?'

'End of the green corridor.'

I thank her and leave, the toilet is empty and has a large window in a minute I'm recovering my carrier bag from the roof and walking back to the *Travellers Rest.*

Whether it's the blood loss or the trek I sleep for a solid twelve hours and thankfully for once I don't dream.

Following morning after a fun hour in the launderette washing the blood out of everything, I go for another full breakfast (although technically its lunch now) and coffee. The waitress keeps the coffee's coming as I take advantage of the free WiFi and google translate.

I've got a good memory for words and I can remember the gist of what mantis said, so it's just working out how to spell it. Imbecile, moron and cretin I can figure out for myself but there was other stuff, tu n'es pas censé être ici is that right? Now that's *you're not supposed to be here,* what did she mean by that? More to the point what the hell is the codex of Estelle? Codex's are wargaming I thought, or very old books, is that what she's looking for?

The name Steven Yardley meant nothing to her I'm sure of that.

I type Codex of Estelle into a search engine and three alarms go off.

Programmers have lots of tricks for dealing with dodgy code one of mine is to run it in a program within a program. It's impossible for anything in the inner program to affect the outer one, anything I'm not sure about I can run knowing that it can't do any real damage.

I'm so used to using it that I've pretty much forgotten that its there but the second I start to look for information about this codex then I get three flags up.

This isn't standard bots or ads these are hunters, self contained programs designed to impregnate my system and report back.

I look at the code as the lovely Michelle brings me another coffee, the code is gorgeous too, really clever, really sophisticated and triggered by something as simple as an entry into a search engine.

What is going on?

There are police everywhere taking statements and asking questions, all of which begin with 'were you here yesterday?'

I tell Karen a pretty PCSO that I've only just arrived and head back to my digs.

I've got a few more days here and I like Cardiff but my time here has left me with more questions than answers.

An hour later I'm back on the train to Paddington.

Protection – Chapter six.

I walk from the station as night falls, I don the costume and return to Greytowers the back way. This is all part of my cunningly conceived plan, my alibi.

There are two entrances/exits to Greytowers, front and back and both on the ground floor. Between these doors is the reception desk manned by Alf. Alf doesn't miss a trick, nobody gets in or out without Alf seeing unless of course they have a super powered alter ego who can climb up and down the corner of the building and then enter/exit through my bathroom window.

The point is I've been home all week and haven't left my flat since I spoke to AlF on Friday night.

I had a food delivery early Friday evening and haven't been out since, if you don't believe me ask Alf.

Whilst isolating I've been doing my job online as Wil will attest. Okay between ourselves I did most of it on a rooftop in the middle of the night whilst I was waiting for La psycho but that's the advantage of working from home.

Now maybe you'll think me paranoid here but if I'd taken a weeks leave in Cardiff and then Any-Man turns up there then even those with the mental acumen of officers James and Hooper are going to make the connection, let alone their boss.

I clamber in through my bathroom window, the fluorescent in Pablo's tank (I have a fish) is the only light but it's enough to see that everything's how I left it.
After a fast shower I grab something that still looks edible from the fridge and a prawn.
The prawn's a treat for Pablo he's a cichlid (Theraps bifasciatum) there's an automated feeder in the hood of his tank but that's just dried tablet food. Pablo loves fresh prawns, well fresh from the fridge, he snatches it from my fingers then chews it enthusiastically as I go to put on the TV in time for the late News.

Guess who's all over the news?

Yep and now the (famously irritable) Home Secretary has got involved, she's glaring at the camera whilst a reporter pokes a thin black microphone up under her nose which makes it look like she's got a moustache.
'How can you say that?' Young Penny the reporter barks with proper outrage. 'Home Secretary we've got costumed Super villains beating each other up whilst your police run around like headless chickens.'

Hang on Super Villains plural?

'Seven of your officers needed hospital treatment,' Penny

continues despite the glare, she's like a ferret squaring up to a lion. 'Whilst the two perpetrators just walk away when they've finished.'

'That is a very *imaginative* account young lady,' the Home Secretary barks back, seriously she is scary. 'But the government has to deal with facts.'

Penny isn't daunted mind. 'Are you suggesting . . ?'

'The fact of the matter is . . .' No the Home Secretary isn't having it, 'An exceptionably well organised and resourced undercover police operation was completely ruined by a costumed thug . . .'

What?

'You mean the Vigilante?'

Any-Man, it's Any-Man!

'Of course I do, let me assure you that there is no such thing as a super powered villain he is just a villain, plain and simple and I assure you that he'll feel the full weight of the law . . .'

'If he hasn't got super powers why haven't you been able to catch him?

I'm liking Penny but super villain come on, I'm hardly Doctor Doom. What's the matter with people?

'He has been extremely fortunate but his luck will run out and when it does . . .'

'Fortune and luck?' Penny's in like a Rottweiler, I'm seriously liking this girl. 'Or incompetence in those whose job it is to bring him in?'

'Police were having to deal with his accomplice . . .'

Accomplice? Oh Mantis will love that!

'The young woman in question was on the very edge of the roof, officers were concerned with her welfare and in trying to keep her safe one of my officers was attacked and thrown off the roof. It's a miracle that she survived, as officers went to her aid they were attacked by the Vigilante.'

I stare at the screen, mouth open, speechless.

'What happened in Cardiff yesterday Penny was that my officers were hospitalised simply because they put the welfare of two costumed thugs and the citizens of the Welsh Capital above their own.'

. . .

'So let me get this clear Home Secretary you're saying that the two of them were working together?'

'Of course.'

'So why is it then that she attacked him?'

'I'm sorry?'

'She attacked him and tried to kill him.'

The Home Secretary is as surprised as I am by this, one of the police must have talked to the press or . . .

'What makes you say that?' The politicians expression and tone is somewhere between annoyance and alarm.

'We have a witness who filmed the entire thing.

The Home Secretary and I both lean forward with similar expressions and interest.

As the reporter holds a laptop up for the Home Secretary to see, the studio show the viewers what she's seeing.

My first thought is that the film has been shot from the helicopter as it's looking down on us but the angles wrong, they must have been on the other side of the roof but how? There were no higher buildings on that side.

The guys are shooting at Mantis, she takes out three from her side then I arrive. The girl falls and I dive after her, Mantis checks the guys on the floor but waits. I come back and she wallops me, fortunately there's no sound but who could have filmed this?

Then the helicopter appears and the camera veers away, it's

only then that it clicks.

It's a drone, you know those little remote control helicopter thingies? You can put cameras on them, someone had one there and filmed everything. I had absolutely no idea, blimey I'm going to be careful when and where I take my mask off in future!

'Well it solves one problem doesn't it Home Secretary?' The camera cuts back to Penny and a clearly seething Home Secretary. 'At least now we can see how the female officer avoided serious injury.'

'Penny that film is evidence it should have . . .'

'It's was only given to us twenty minutes ago Home Secretary and of course we sent a copy directly to the police.'

'Even so . . .'

'The film clearly shows that it was the Vigilante who rescued your officer . . .'

YES! Way to go Penny, I love this girl, she should be nominated for a services to journalism award, who do I have to contact?

'And isn't this what is really upsetting you Home Secretary, the Vigilante was clearly trying to stop Mantis, as so many people are saying he's doing the work that you and your police are failing to do.'

Maybe an Oscar or a Bafta, do they give those to journalists?

'True, she overcame him easily and he's clearly no match for her . . .'

Steady on now.

'But far from being a villain, out to make trouble he's simply trying to prop up a system that is all too clearly failing.'
'Penny what kind of concerned citizen puts on a grotesque mask and goes around beating up . . .'
'Thugs and hooligans, money lenders, pimps and enforcers.'
Penny interrupts, her knuckles white around her microphone as I will her on.
'This is Britain,' the Home secretary gasps matching the young reporter's outrage. 'We are a civilised country, we have the finest judicial system and the best police force in the world . . .'
'Both of which have been cut to the bone!'
'Look at what's happening in the world, look at what this country has been through, it's not for Government to throw more money . . .
There's a loud rap on the door.
'It's open,' I shout, knowing full well who it is.
'What the hell were you doing in Cardiff?' Adam saunters in carrying a large plain carrier bag. 'There was nothing about

it in your blog.'

'Haven't had chance to write it up yet,' I lie effortlessly rubbing my hair dry with the towel. 'There's lager in the fridge.'

Adam heads for the fridge, the kitchen is basically a small corner off the large open plan living room. He grabs two cans and a prawn.

'He's just had one.'

Adam gives Pablo another prawn regardless, 'you know you can put a catfish in with him, those one's that eat the algae off the glass.'

'Plecostomus,' I tell him.

Adam grins, 'see you are remembering stuff.' He passes me a tin and drops into the armchair opposite.

'Just not the stuff that matters.' I open the tin and take a sip, 'everything else is fine it's just the dream . . .'

'Embedded nightmare son,' he tells me pointing his can at me. 'Let it go, the more you dwell on it the more real it becomes, I did tell you.'

'You told me I supported Arsenal.'

Adam laughs, choking on a mouthful of lager.

During my rehab he took me to the Emmirates saying that I, like he, was a life long Arsenal fan. Problem was the game was against City and every time that City scored I was on my feet cheering, like it was a reflex. It didn't exactly endear me to the home supporters I can tell you!

I look Adam up and down, he's changed quite a bit. He always used to be smart, his hair and his clothes, I even thought he was gay at one point, not that he ever tried anything.

Now he looks tired, worn, his shirt hasn't been ironed and there's a stain on his tie, he's not himself somehow.

'You okay mate?'

'Never better,' he answers quickly grinning at the Home Secretary squirming in close up. 'So come on lets have it.'

'What?'

'Your blog old son has become a tad boring of late, you go to work, have lunch, back to work, have supper, go out slap a thug then bed.'

'Mate you said write everything down, it all just becomes routine after a while.'

'Yeah?' Adam takes another sip then points to the telly. 'So you just happened to be in Cardiff?'

I tell him about my trip and the lengths I went to cover it.

'So how strong was she?' He asks fascinated.

'Far stronger than normal but it was her speed that was the problem.'

'She was faster than you?' Adam asks raising his eyebrows.

'You can't really tell from the film it's all just a blur but she didn't miss you by much.'

I pull a face, 'she didn't *miss* me at all mate!' I roll up the sleeve of my sweatshirt and show Adam my arm.

His turn to pull a face.

'She cut you twice?'

'No the long one was her, the other one was from the bank job last week.'

'What bank Job!?'

'Didn't I mention that in the blog?'

This is the problem with keeping a secret blog beside the main one.

'No you bloody didn't!'

'Oh right, well there wasn't too much to it in truth, some guys were knocking over a building society . . .'

'Armed?'

'Only shotguns.'

'*Only* shotguns?'

'So I knocked them over.'

'And the arm?'

'Jumped through a window didn't I?'

'You pillock!'

'Aw come on, how many times have you seen Spider-Man or Daredevil jump through a window?' I protest.

Adam shakes his head with a slightly disappointed look.

'So the stitches?'

'Local nurse after the building society, turned up in her

office in costume and she stitched me up without a word.'

'And Cardiff?'

'Bit more complicated, lost the helicopter in one of their arcades then got a taxi to the local A&E.'

'What in costume?' Adam looks at me properly horrified.

'No you pillock, I covered my arm and told him that my kid had been taken in. When I got there, there were builders working in the grounds I told the nurse I was one of them and the angle grinder had slipped.'

Adam smirks, 'what name did you use?'

'Terry Wait.'

'Oh he'll love that.'

'Adam *if* they do follow it up he's five foot five and seven stone, he's obviously not me.'

'If the police do realise that you were injured they'll ask the local hospitals.' Adam replies slowly, thinking hard.

'And the best they'll manage is a description of an average looking guy of my height and build. The Sister was too busy rowing with the receptionist to even look at me properly, you know how busy they are.'

'Even so, she did see you, she could give them an excellent description for all you know.'

'I doubt it,' I tell him with a smile after another sip, 'you should see the description they've got of me in police HQ down the road, six foot six and . . .'

I'm halted by Adam's horrified expression, 'what were you

doing in police HQ?'

'When they took me in for questioning,' I answer lamely.

'THEY DID WHAT?'

'Didn't I mention it in the blog?'

There's a great deal of swearing at this point which we'll skip over as I can't spell most of it.

I explain and calm Adam down but he's clearly not happy.

'The point is mate,' I tell him quietly, 'even trained police officers describe me as far taller and larger than I am. Six foot six come on that's half a foot out. It's your costume mate it . . .'

'Stephen you must be careful.'

'I am mate but what I'm doing can't always be done quietly.'

Adam sighs, glancing at the Telly where Penny is doing her signing off piece to camera.

I go and get Adam another lager as he crumples up his can and lobs it towards the bin in the kitchen. 'What was she like then, apart from fast?'

'Gorgeous mate,' I pick his can up from the floor and drop it into the bin then pass him another. 'And French.'

'French?' Adam asks with surprise.

'Pas étonnant que tu aies des bandages sur la tête ont-ils enlevé votre cerveau.'

'Go on?'

'No wonder you've got bandages on your head, did they

remove your brain?'

Adam laughs and I laugh with him.

'So what was she looking for?'

'No idea mate,' I lie and I'm not sure why, maybe I am becoming paranoid.

'So did you ask her out?'

'Mantis?!'

'Helen.'

I sigh, 'no mate.'

'And why might that be?'

'Because I feel like . . . like I belong to somebody else.'

Adam leans forward with his best concerned look, 'how many times mate, your re-enforcing doubts and notions that have no basis in reality. I went over your records mate, there was nobody, you were a loner and Stephen you must have realised by now mate, nobody's looking.'

I nod slowly.

'You're hanging on to hopes and ideas, dreams of the life that you wanted for yourself and you're missing out on real life.' He pauses for a sip of lager. 'You're making your life for yourself, you've done great with the job but there's nobody waiting for you mate, nobody looking.'

I nod again.

'Ask her out, take her to the cinema, promise me?'

'There's this really nice nurse as well, Mary she's called she's bloody gorgeous mate!' I tell him quietly.

'That's my boy!' Adam leans forward and slaps me on the shoulder, 'sorry that was the bad one wasn't it?'

'Don't worry.'

'What kind of films does Mary like?'

'No idea.'

'So find out.'

'Promise?'

'I will,' I tell him, deliberately neglecting to mention that it was Mary who patched me up after the bank. 'And I'll try and keep up with the blog.'

'So?'

'So?'

'So aren't you going to ask me why I'm here?'

'I knew as soon as me and Mantis made the news you'd be over.' I tell him getting myself a second tin from the fridge.

'Hey that's a point if the stories just broken on the news how did you . . .'

Adam laughs he's clearly happier now and much more like his old self.

'That clip was from the lunchtime news they showed it over for the evening news and over again now for the late news. You and super chic have been on the news all day.'

'Seriously?'

'And what do you suppose your man in Havana, your agent Q does when he sees his boy getting a kicking from super bitch?'

'What have you done Adam?'

'White bag by the door.'

'I'm in the bag in a second.'

'And?'

'Well it's a green metal bar, one inch diameter best part of two feet long and it's er . . . green.' I hold it up, turning and weighing it in my hand.

'And?'

'Well it's a very nice green metal bar Adam, the green's the same as the green on the costume so I'm guessing that it's my green bar but oh wait . . .'

'There's a button at the bottom.'

'There's a button at the bottom,' I press the button pointing the bar at the open window. 'Nothing happened was it supposed to . . .'

Adam picks up a small picture in a steel frame off the table and throws it at me. It sticks to the bar with a clang.

'The button magnetises it.'

'The button magnetises it.' Adam repeats with a smug smile. 'She comes at you with blades, you can't fight her with your hands, she'll cut you to ribbons. Steel's magnetic anyway and Japanese weapon makers traditionally favour iron-rich sand to produce their steel.'

'You're an expert on Japanese weapon making techniques now?'

'You've heard of the internet right?'

'Go on.'

'So Samurai swords are about speed and sharpness, if you concentrate on achieving those you do so at the expense of strength and durability. You make the blade hard you get the speed and the edge but you make the blade more brittle. If she swings a sword at you, you meet the blade with that! It's Nandermol, mid secret military spec . . .'

'Mid secret?'

'One down from top secret, it's one of the composites they use in modern tank armour. That bar is worth three grand so don't lose it.'

I whistle in appreciation, 'where did you get it?'

'Fell off the back of a Challenger two. Now it's a tube with a circuit inside, when you switch it on it becomes a magnet it'll hold her blade.' Adam takes the bar off me, 'say her blade is stuck like this,' Adam demonstrates with his free hand. 'You then turn the bar back on the blade like this and . . .'

'She drops the blade or I shatter her wrist.'

Adam nods, 'also if you're fencing with her your advantage is brute force, her blade will be around a quarter of an inch thick you've got what is in effect a beefed up iron bar, it's four times the cross section. Bring it down on the blade at an angle,' he demonstrates with his arm again, 'and I'm betting you'll break her blade.'

'Superb!'

'Put two loops on the back of a leg on the costume or you

115

can hang it from a belt. Then there's these.'

Adam pulls out what looks like a small cage. Two metal rings, the upper one is slightly larger than the lower one, connected by thin metal rods each the thickness of a pencil. 'Put your arm through the rings.'
I do as I'm told seeing there's another in the bag.
'See it covers your lower arm from your wrist to your elbow, magnet button by there look. It gives you the option to block her blade with your forearms. She can't thrust her blade through into your arm when the magnets are on because the point of the blade will just stick to the nearest one.'
'You've knocked these up since lunchtime?' I ask him incredulously.
'TA mate, always ready, always prepared.'
'These are great, now I just need a cover story for a return trip to Cardiff . . .'
'Don't!' Adam's face is serious again, 'I didn't make these so you could go after her, I made them to protect you if she comes here.'
'But . . .'
'Stephen think about it, you've got an alibi, you were in your flat all week but you've also got two properly distinctive scars on your arm, that alone rules out T shirts for the foreseeable.'
'Yes but . . .'

'Now the police are going to examine that film, they'll slow it down and they'll see that her blade caught you, first thing they'll do then is talk to the local hospitals. The hospital will have already realised by now that you gave them a false name and you're not with the builders on site. Now they probably won't bother to contact the police but when the police contact them you can guarantee they'll tell them all they know.'

'But there's no link back to me and neither was there any CCTV in the hospital.' I point out, 'all they'll have is a nurse's description of Joe average.'

'Your blood will be on the roof, they'll get DNA from it, you're fortunate yours is not on their database.' Adam replies thinking hard. 'Don't go giving them any reason to take samples whatever you do.'

I nod.

'Point is you've got to be more careful, more discrete . . .'

'Discrete?' I laugh, 'you do remember the mask that *you* designed don't you?'

'Just stay local, if super bitch comes here you can handle her now but don't go looking for her.'

I nod. 'She's no reason to come here mate.' I tell him but Adam's expression suggests that he doesn't seem so sure.

'You think she might?'

'Edinburgh and Cardiff.'

'Yep so?'

'They're both capitals mate, Scotland and Wales.'

'Ah fair point, I didn't think of that, still it's a bit thin mate.'

'Aye,' Adam agrees, then another thought strikes him. 'You saw the Home Secretary's face right?'

'Aye, it was a picture.' I tell him with a giggle.

'Agreed, but . . .'

'But?'

'Mate, she was absolutely livid, she's just been shown up on national television, soon as she's back in her office she's gonna be on the phone screaming at every police chief in the area. They'll demand resources and this time now its personal and she *will* find them. If anything Steve, you should lay low for a while.'

'You think?'

'Yeah keep your head down for a bit, take Anne . . .'

'Mary.'

'Take Mary to the cinema, or Helen, or both of them.'

'Of yeah cos that can't go wrong.'

Adam drops his empty can into the bin and turns for the door.

'What, are you going?'

'I need an early night.'

'It was Spurs Arsenal earlier, the battle for fourth, I recorded it, want to watch, I don't know the score.'

Adams expression tells me at once that he does know the score and that he doesn't want to watch.'

'Like that was it?'

'Good night Stephen.' And he's gone.

I drop back into my chair and grab the lager. The news is now telling me that another two vagrants have disappeared without a trace. That's six in a week but my mind is turning over all that Adam said.

He called Mary, Anne. It was a slip, the sort of mistake you'd make when somebody has got a new girlfriend. I noticed because he's done it before. A month ago he asked me about Anne in the office after I'd mentioned Helen previously. But the name Anne doesn't ring any bells or feel familiar in anyway. Maybe I really am becoming paranoid.

Pablo playfully head butts the glass which is his signal for I'd like another prawn please. With my sternest expression I remind him that he's already had two tonight.

Then there was all that stuff about the police record, I'm sure you noticed as well and you'll remember that he told me originally that I was always in trouble with the police as a youngster. If that were true then they would have detailed records but I already know that they don't (yep I searched the police database.)

Then there's the gear, you can't just walk out of an army compound with bits of a tank surely?

The arm guards look purpose made, there's no way these were knocked up by an amateur in an afternoon.

But then the other side of this is pretty much everything else he told me makes complete sense and he's obviously trying to help.

I head to the fridge for another beer and a prawn and can't help laughing as Pablo pulls it out of my fingers.

I drop back on the chair beside the table where Adam sat; it's a good job he didn't look at it closely as I hadn't shut it properly last time.

The table is actually a desk, the flat top is actually a lid, when raised it stands at a ninety degree angle to the desk and is in effect a large notice board. I've got it laid out like a police incident board, like you see on the telly a map of the area with suspects and clues lined up around it on all sides.

There is no way that I'm forgetting the dream, instead I've been doing the opposite.

I think it's called a waking dream, unlike a normal dream where you're just carried along by events, in mine I've got control, I can make decisions. It always starts in the same place and ends in the same way but I can choose my route. Think of a computer game. You're going to end up getting killed by the boss in the corridor but where you go beforehand and what you do is down to you.

It begins inside the bloody cabinet, in the past it was a struggle to get out but now it's a piece of cake.

Then soon as I'm out I've started to look around properly,

I've measured the morgue, paced it out, then soon as I'm awake I write it all down in a notebook I keep beside the bed.
In this way I've built up a proper map and drawn a detailed plan.

There's a central corridor, three small offices and the morgue. The morgue and one of the offices has been ransacked but everywhere else is normal.
There's paperwork all over the floor of the ransacked office and there's a filing cabinet on its side. There's broken glass over the floor of the morgue, a broken window and dozens of broken bottles, all with coloured glass and all either green or blue or yellow.
Of late my interest has been in the clothes on the floor, I've tried to list them accurately because they're the key to something I'm sure of it.
The problem is my time is limited and the second I see the monster that's it. My reaction is always the same, I am completely terrified, it shambles towards me arms outstretched and I scream like a baby. Next second I'm sat up in bed in a cold sweat reaching for the notebook.
I go and grab the notebook as Pablo tries to attract my attention again. Then I carefully add the contents of the latest list to the one beside the plan.
There were three others beside me, I'm sure now. There were

at least seven trainers that I could see on the floor, one pair were mine but there was another pair that I knew, they were familiar somehow. White trainers with red laces, too small for me but familiar none the less.

Four pairs of jeans, two of them slashed down the side, mine I recognised from the belt but there was no wallet in my pocket. It should have been in the back left I thought and that's where I carry mine now but it wasn't there.

There's a pile of underwear that includes a bra and four T shirts, three have been slashed down the side. I pull on the only one that's still intact, it's not mine.

Whatever happened, it happened to four of us but I was the only one there, me and that thing and before you ask, yes I checked the other drawers in the cabinet but it was just me. I stare at the plan for a full hour before calling it a night and taking the notebook to bed with me.

Stan the man – Chapter seven

The following morning I ring Wil to tell him I'll be in for work.

'Excellent,' He booms, 'when did you test clear?'

'This morning,' I tell him.

'And Yesterday?'

'Er . . . nope, the line was faint mind.'

'Got to test clear twice *completely* clear for two days old son.'

'Ah . . .'

'No worries I've got a courier on their way round to you with a laptop it's from Crooks the estate agent, it keeps trying to reformat itself.'

'Sweet.'

'She took it home and her little 'un smeared Jam all over the keyboard.'

'Oh great!'

'Do you think you'll be able to sort it?'

'Depends, what type of jam was it?'

'I think she said strawberry, does that make any . . . you're joking aren't you?' Wil sighs.

'Yep, I'll see what I can do with it and bring it back in tomorrow.'

I wait an hour for the courier, then sort out the laptop which is much easier to do than I suspected.

Bored then I head down to the basement parking level to give the car a run. Upon my return I see the legend that is Stan, the man, Stanhope.

Now Stan is in his seventies, he's a typical biker, built like a brick outhouse and boasting a formidable white handlebar moustache.

His pride and joy is an ancient Triumph 400 motorbike which you can hear coming a mile away.

Stan nursed his wife of forty years through Alzheimers and the general consensus when she passed was that he wasn't going to be too far behind her.

Not a bit of it, it was apparently as if Stan got a new lease of life. Every day and every evening he was out, I don't think there's a single female pensioner within five miles of Greytowers who hasn't gone out with Stan at some point. Seeing me park in the bay opposite his he comes over to see me.

'I've been trying to get you all week son, there's been no answer.'

'Sorry Stan, I've had the bug mate, not felt too bad but had my headphones on cos they sent work round for me.' I lie calmly and with an affable expression.

'No worries son, I just wanted to ask you a question.'

'Go for it.'

'Can you ride a motorbike?'

Now the simple answer is I honestly don't know but I can hardly say that now can I? I go with, 'never tried mate.'

'Right hop on Bessie.'

'What?' I gasp, 'are you serious? Mate I'd be too worried about denting your bike.' I reply, completely genuine for once.

'C'mon she's a pussycat, come and get your leg over.' He answers with his best smile.

To cut a longish story short, within quarter of an hour or so I'm riding Bessie confidently around the parking lot. I'm confident because it feels familiar.

'Lying toe rag,' Stan Chuckles, 'don't you tell me that's your first time on a bike, you can't kid a kidder son.'

'Stan she's wonderful, so responsive, I can't believe she's as old as she is.'

'Oy, wash your mouth out, don't you use language like that in front of her!'

I laugh and stop the bike beside him, turning the key off and easing the bike up on its stand.

'Why do I sense that there's an ulterior motive here Stan?'

'Because you're a smart lad and there is.'

'Go on.'

Stan pulls a photo out of his wallet and hands it to me.

'Blimey she's . . .'

'My daughter.'

'Nice, she looks very nice.'

Stan smirks, 'not seen her since before this bug started, she's in Australia, Queensland, she wants me to stay with her for a couple of months.'

I chuckle and hand him back the picture, 'and you want somebody to look after Bessie for you?'

He grins back, 'Just give her a run, once a week or a fortnight, the further the better. Keeps everything ticking over if I leave her standing she'll just seize up.'

'Sounds good to me, I can insure her with the car.'

'No I'm not having you paying anything, I'll put you as named driver on mine, you can ride her on L plates. There are two magnetic ones in the box behind the saddle.

I cheerfully give him my details then he presents me with his old battered white crash helmet and the keys.

So why am I going into so much detail about this?

Because it is all extremely fortuitous that's why and the timing is perfect.

I head off into town on foot to the nearest motorbike centre where a plump girl with a pretty face and gorgeous smile comes to my assistance.

'I'm Cheryl,' she tells me, 'how can I help?'

'Hi Cheryl, I'm looking to buy a Birthday present for a mate, he wants a black crash helmet with a full-face dark visor.'

'How much do you want to spend?' She asks me with a knowing smile.

Stan tells me that I'll be insured from midnight and at five past midnight I'm loose.

The jacket's reversed so it's just a black bikers jacket and with the black helmet I'm just another motorbike.

In no time at all I see a disturbance outside a chip shop, now if it was a fair fight I'd leave it be but this obviously isn't.

There's a guy and his girlfriend trying to walk away and three guys that aren't letting them.

I stop the bike and pull it up onto its stand and stamp over towards them pulling the visor down over my face.

The nearest seeing me coming turns and pulls a knife from his pocket. 'Nothing to do with you boy, walk away or I'll cut you.' He points the knife in my direction.

I grab the hand that holds the knife and squeeze it hard enough to audibly break his fingers, he drops to the floor with a squeal.

His mate leaps at me but I catch him lifting him off the floor and hurling him to the side, his feet catch the man sobbing on his knees as he flies into him and he lands heavily on both knees with a scream.

The third guy tries to run for it but I catch him and upend him, ramming him head down into a large concrete bin full of mildewed chips and vomit. His shoulders catch on the sides as I ram him down, he's jammed solid both of his legs sticking up into the air.

'You're not local?' I ask the couple, like nothing's happened.

'Hereford, we came over for a show.' The girl tells me with a sweet smile.

'Best stay in the City Centre where its busy,' I advise.

'We got lost looking for a chippie.' The guy says raising his voice over the shouting of the guy that's stuck in the bin and the sobbing of the two on the pavement.

'I'm calling the police,' the old guy behind the counter in the chippie shouts out holding up his phone.

'Shame you didn't do that earlier when these two were being threatened.' I shout back.

I direct the couple to the right road and reclaim Bessie, I find out afterwards that it takes the fire brigade two hours to get the guy out of the bin.

I drive home picking a route with the minimum of cameras, both number plates have *somehow* got covered in mud anyway. On the way back I see a house burglar who, after a chase, I throw off the adjoining roof.

All in all its been a good evening, Any-Man (or the Vigilante delete as you choose) has been keeping his head down whilst London's underworld have not been having it all their own way.

On Thursday I go around to see Emma, I've got a nagging feeling she was trying to tell me something but she's not in. It's raining and London's quiet so I head home with a Chinese meal.

I'm eating it off a tray on my lap and switch on the telly for the news, five black and white mug shots fill the screen and the reporter's voice over gets my immediate attention.

Peter Drew was one of the junior members of the gang, he was inside the building society and rendered unconscious by the Vigilante. From there and following medical attention he was detained in Sunnybank remand centre pending trial.

The screen switches to a wide-angled shot of the remand centre, a 1970's breeze block construct which suggests that the design brief had made frequent mention of the word drab. The reporter's voice continues in the background-

Mr Drew was not considered high risk but even so as these pictures show Sunnybank is clearly a secure and well protected facility. The compound is patrolled by officers with dogs and you can see the height of the fence for yourselves. The managers here maintain that his breakout was highly organised which is extremely surprising given the criminals lowly status.

The camera switches to the studio and a concerned looking reporter behind his microphone.

'Although the centre's management were reluctant to speak to us this reporter was able to talk with one or two of the inmates who were working in the garden outside.'

He pauses for dramatic effect, eyes on the camera. 'These men told me a completely different story. They were adamant that rather than a highly skilled military-style underworld operation to free the man what actually happened was the terrified prisoner was dragged screaming from his cell. A single figure carried him with one hand and, if these witnesses are to be believed, walked up a wall and onto the roof carrying off the hapless Mr Drew with him.'

The camera returns to the centre and begins a slow zoom towards a roof top.

As incredible as all this sounds, when questioned Sunnybank management did eventually confirm that large amounts of Mr Drew's blood were found upon the roof top and now tonight this reporter is able to tell you that there has been another incredible twist to this developing story.

It seems that only a week or so ago another member of this same gang a Mr Steven Yardley was also abducted from another

government facility and this time brutally murdered in the process.
Authorities refused to give details but a source told us that the
man's injuries were consistent with having been run over by a
train or a tank.

We did ask the Home Office for a statement but were told that
nobody was available. A spokesman however was prepared to tell
us that the remaining members of the gang were moved to a secret
location as a precaution.

The camera cuts back to another concerned face, that of
Steve the news anchor.

'Are they blaming the Vigilante for this Robert?' Steve asks
shaking his head, the camera cuts to an, extremely bad,
artists impression of my mask.

'Not this time Steven, he brought them in as you remember
and he certainly ruffed them up a bit but he it seems was
more interested in rescuing the cashier.'

The camera cuts to the girl from the building society, Angela
the caption tells me. It was obviously filmed earlier as she's
outside in the sunlight.

'He was so brave, he just stood there laughing and all their
bullets were bouncing off him. Then he jumps on 'em, gives
them a right kicking, then he scoops me up in his arms and
takes me out the back and checks I'm alright.'

'Did you feel unsafe?' Penny's there with her microphone,
'alone with a masked man?'

'No he was really gentle, you can see his eyes and I could just tell the way he was looking at me, you know sometimes when your eyes meet?'

Penny nods breathlessly.

'I just knew I had nothing to fear. It was a really special moment, if you know what I mean.' Angela blushes slightly.

'What happened next?' Penny thrusts her microphone back at the girl.

'Well the building fell down and the police were yelling and shouting outside telling me to get on my knees and crawl over broken glass.'

'Did the Vigilante seem particularly interested in the gun men?'

'Not at all, he just gave them a slap, he was more interested in me to be honest.' Angela bats her eyelashes staring wistfully into the camera.

'Well there we are,' Penny turns back to the camera with her microphone under her nose. 'It seems that the Vigilante was more interested in the girl than the gang.' Penny grins, adjusting her microphone. 'So whether it's a cashier in London or a masked sword wielding psychopath in Cardiff it looks like we've found this particular Super Villains weakness.'

I stare at my telly open-mouthed and lost for words.

Back to Steven in the studio, 'so if it's not the Vigilante are there any suggestions that the Mantis is behind this Robert?' 'No not this time, it seems whilst this was happening in London, Mantis had broken into Cardiff central library, nothing was taken but she was picked up on their CCTV.' Steven turns back to the camera slowly shaking his head, 'what strange times we live in,' the music and credits start. 'Good night.'

I stare at the telly gobsmacked for a few more moments.

There's obviously two things going on at the moment that may or may not be related.

I've got a really strong feeling that Emma knows more than she's letting on about the one but there's not a lot I can do about that until I can catch up with her.

A phone call from Wil interrupts my deliberations, and like the bike it proves fortuitous.

See I'd been looking for that codex on line and was getting nowhere fast, until I looked to see why I was getting nowhere fast.

They're called erasers or killers, they're bots that roam the internet wiping out references to specific things. They're generally low level and thwarted by most of the security stuff that's out there but occasionally you come across some properly high level ones. We're talking state sponsored terrorism here. Your country is attracting a lot of bad press because of your appalling human rights so you hack the internet and re-write it or remove it anything that's negative. The security services have got guys fighting wars against this sort of thing.

Well it turns out that somebody, somewhere, doesn't want anybody finding out anything about the codex of Estelle and they've got the resources to acquire high level aps.

Now the problem with these is that they can cope with really advanced detection software and still cause havoc but they'll quite often miss the low level stuff.

For example a fisherman in Newport digging for bait finds a steel trunk buried in the grounds of a stately house. Inside is an old book, the index to the codex Estelle, he tries to sell it and claims that masked men took it off him at gunpoint.

It made the local paper, the South Wales Argus but not the Nationals consequently the story escaped their bots but not mine.

So why is Wil's call fortuitous?

Well after a little digging I discover that Paul Campbell the guy who dug up the trunk is still alive and living near Cambridge.

Now Wil is sending me to Oxford tomorrow for a conference

and although I've never been to Oxford or Cambridge before (as far as I know) I do know that they're close (they race boats with each other.)

I'll take the car rather than the train then once the conference is over I'll tootle over to Cambridge and have a chat to Mr Campbell.

Okay, the following day I get to discover a couple of things. Firstly Oxford and Cambridge are NOT next door to each other or even remotely close. Secondly North Norfolk (where Mr Campbell lives) is not Cambridge.

The satnav finds the conference centre (and its extremely expensive parking) and I'm straight into the first 90 minute lecture which is computer security. It can best be summed up with the phrase *stating the blindly bloody obvious.* After that its refreshments with my fellow geeks then two more lectures (these fortunately are much more interesting) and we get to go home at three.

The real value of this part of the day is the contacts I make. There's a hacking group called Chrysalis, they're hackers with a conscience. They've all done well in the industry and want to give back. So they target crime and local government misdemeanours. I've had dealings with them before online but it's nice to put faces to names. One of them, a skinny guy with the biggest beard you've ever seen is called Max. A fortnight ago he showed me how to use what looked like a virus to send the *wrong* set of files to the guys (another loan shark) entire email list.

To everyone concerned it would just look like the guy had picked up a virus on line which had randomly sent a file to everybody on his email list. It just so happened that the file was his hidden accounts and one of the organisations on his email list was the Tax office.

It just looked like the guy had been unlucky rather than hacked.

With the people that these hackers target it's better not to leave any traces of your activity.

Max and I chat over a pint and he introduces me to a handful of other programmers all of whom are in Chrysalis and I get invited to their monthly online D&D meetings.

Incidentally you're probably thinking that it will be impossible to keep a blog like this secret when so many of your mates are hackers but I've got that covered.

There's one foolproof way of keeping your documents safe, put them into a computer that's not online!

This one doesn't even have a modem, I'm just writing it all down cos it helps. I'll probably delete it all at the end, that or change the names and details and email the whole thing to one of those Indy authors.

Anyway I'm out of Oxford and on the LONG and difficult drive to Cambridge, road works and queues, you know the drill.

I'm looking for a village called Syderstone, which it turns out is miles from Cambridge.

North Norfolk for the uninitiated looks like England did in the 1950's, lots of flint cottages in pretty villages, each of which has its own ornate name sign, duck pond, pub and church. It is gorgeous here, like going back in time, I'm expecting to see Miss Marple coming around the corner by the letterbox. It's hard to believe that this is the same country as London.

I stop at a pub called the Lost Angel and have the best Shepherd's pie that I've had in my life (that I can remember.)

Finally I'm pulling up outside Paul Campbell's cottage, (having had to stop and ask directions twice despite the satnav.)

The cottage has seen better days, flaking paint on the woodwork, a cracked window and an abandoned freezer lying across the front of the house, partially obscuring the front door.

I walk down the path and ring the bell, a shadow appears behind the small grimy window in the middle of the door.

'Who's there?'

'Mr Campbell, Mr Paul Campbell?'

'Aye, what do you want?'

'Mr Campbell you don't know me, my name is Stephen Bishop I'm looking for information about the codex of Estelle but I'm getting nowhere fast. I found your name . . .' I stop as the door opens an inch with a crack. I see a strip of tired lined face and a bright blue eye.

'You genuine?'

'I am Paul,' I promise you.'

He opens the door slowly, like his cottage he's seen better days, his clothes are grubby and his skin appears to be slightly too big for him but his eyes are bright and keen.

'Sorry bout that fridge,' he says gruffly. 'I put it out for the scrappy but they can't take e'm no more cos of the gas. Then it fell over and I can't move it.'

'Where do you want it?' I ask cheerfully.

'Well round the side if you could,' he nods towards the side of the house. 'But you won't shift that on your own.'

'I'm stronger than I look,' I tell him with a smile as I grab the freezer in the middle and lift it, I take it around the side making it look like it's a struggle.

'Do you want these sleepers sorted out whilst I'm here,' I shout back to him. There's a pile of old railway sleepers that has obviously fallen over.

'Well if you could lad.'

In no time I've got the sleepers stacked tidily and the freezer standing up against the wall.

'That's not going to fall over now,' I tell him. 'But what will you do with it?'

'I'll get the council to come and take it when I've got a couple of quid.' He tells me grinning from ear to ear as he surveys my handiwork.

'Right lad, I'd say you've earned yourself a drink, come inside, I'll get the kettle on then I'll tell you all about that blasted book.'

Paul moves his cat so I've got an armchair to myself, the cat, white all over with green eyes clearly doesn't approve of this or me. It leaps up onto my knee and stares into my eyes, if looks could kill.

'Tea or coffee,' Paul shouts cheerfully from the kitchen.

'Whatever you're making mate.'

'Milk and sugar.'

'Both please, two sugars.'

Paul bustles about in the kitchen as his cat plans his next move.

Soon he appears with a tray, there's two steaming mugs of tea and a plate of chocolate hobnobs.

'Can I ask your interest in the codex,' Paul hands me my tea then offers me a biscuit as the cat curls up on my lap.

'I'm a computer programmer Paul,' I tell him helping myself to a biscuit, 'and I don't like things that I can't understand. There is software on the internet, really advanced, really clever and its wiping out every mention of the codex and I want to know why.'

Paul settles himself back into his settee which is opposite me, he takes a thoughtful sip of his tea. 'Do you know Newport lad?'

'It's down the M4 from Cardiff,' I reply, 'on the Bristol channel.'

He nods, 'I'm from there originally, from the Gaer, it's an estate on the West of the river.'

I nod, although I've never been to Newport (at least I don't think I have.)

I used to help out at a Youth club, they were good to me when I was a kid so when I grew . . .'

'You helped out to give something back.' I guess between sips.

'Well there were lot of poverty there, loads of kids with nothing, so we used to take em' fishing. Down the docks in the winter and Tredegar house in the summer.'

'Big country house and gardens,' I tell him snapping my fingers, it was on the Antiques Road show the other night.

'Aye that's it,' he smiles back and passes me another biscuit.

'You're not allowed to fish either now mind, there's even less places for the kids to go, no wonder they hang about on street corners making trouble.'

'It was there you found the trunk?'

'Aye, see it were Tomo's turn to bring the bait but he'd put the maggots in the fridge and he'd not put the top down proper.'

I laugh, guessing the rest. 'This was 1974 right?'

He nods, 'now his Mrs went mental and threw out the lot.'

'So you had no bait?'

'I took half a loaf with me but we needed more so I went on a wander with an empty bait tub. See there's woods all around the lake, I found a fallen tree, there were loads of grubs and such under the bark, then I had a dig around in the soil with my knife where the roots had been.'

'And you found the trunk.'

'It were only small, fourteen inches across but a proper little trunk with hinges and a lock.'

'And inside was the book?'

'Aye, the lock was bust and inside wrapped in cloth was the book. It were a Victorian notebook, a little smaller than A4 written across the front it said Index codex de Estelle a copy by Adorabella Manning.'

'So it was a Victorian copy of an older book?'

'Aye that's what I figured.'

'Did you read it?'

Paul bursts out laughing, tipping some of his tea down his front. 'Read it?' he chuckles, 'ain't no one could read it.'

'Go on.'

'Well it were all gobbledygook weren't it, just numbers and letters. You know the old log books they had in school before computers?'

'Aye,' I know what he means.

'Well it were like that, thirty three pages of letters and numbers, hundreds of them.' Paul tells me wiping his front with his sleeve before taking another sip.

'So it was some kind of code?'

'Aye that's what I figured.'

I nod slowly, 'okay what happened then?'

'Well see Newport had a great big indoor market, I had a stall there between the comics and books up stairs. Antiques and odds and ends. We all used to send lists of what we had to the larger stores and specialists.'

'So you put the book on the list?'

'Aye,' Paul tells me nodding mournfully. 'Then following Saturday when I turn up there's this fella waiting for me. Have you got the book he says, I show it to him, how much? He says without even opening it. Twenty five I tell him and he gives me the money there and then.'

'Then what?'

'Well see rest of the day I'm thinking I should have charged him more but still twenty five quid for something that's cost me nowt. Anyways I pack up come five, it were Autumn so it were dark so I was carrying my stuff round to my Imp in the car park and these guys jumped me and stuffed me in the back of a jag. Next thing I know I'm on the floor outside a scrap yard getting a right kicking, it were round the back of the Octopus bridge in Pill. Then they dragged me to a railway workers hut and made me tell them everything. They made me tell them over and over, then they poured whiskey all over me and beat me unconscious.' I can hear the emotion in his voice and know beyond doubt that he's

143

genuine.

'What about the police?'

'I told them what had happened but you could see they didn't believe me and in the end it was me that got done for wasting their time, that's how I got in the paper.'

I tut and shake my head.

'The sergeant told me that he'd talked to a witness who said I'd been wandering around the pubs with a bottle trying to start a fight.'

'Did he give you the name of the witness?'

Paul shakes his head.

I finish my tea thinking quietly as the cat snores loudly on my lap.

'Paul has anybody else asked you about the book?'

His face creases into a wide smile, 'aye good job you said I'd have forgotten. He puts his cup down and heads for a battered sideboard covered with neatly folded newspapers. He pulls open a drawer and starts to rummage through its contents.

'Mrs Sandra Dobson, Oxford university.' He hands me her business card.

I smirk, taking the card. 'That's typical isn't it?' I tell him taking a photo of the card with my phone. 'I was in Oxford this morning.' I hand him back the card.

'Did she tell you anything about the book?'

'No, she said she had an interest in old books but her card

says she's a biologist. She were nice enough and she talked a lot, she just didn't tell me anything.'

'She wasn't French was she?'

'Nope, Humberside born and bred.' Paul shakes his head.

I finish my tea and rise slowly, lifting the snoring cat from my lap and lowering it onto the cushion.

'Listen Paul you've been a big help. 'Here,' I pull forty quid in notes out of my pocket. 'That's for the council to move your fridge.'

'Oh lad, there's no need for you to do that.'

'Paul I insist,' I tell him handing him the cash. 'You're the only person I've talked to who's been any help.' He takes the money and I offer him my other hand.

He grasps it shaking it firmly. 'If you find out more will you let me know?'

'Are you sure you want me too?' I ask quietly. 'Are you sure you want to know?'

He nods solemnly.

'Then I'll keep you in the loop, do you have an email address?'

He laughs aloud.

'Okay I'll send a postcard, I know your address.'

We head for the door.

'Did you ever go back? Newport I mean.'

'Nah, family and friends disowned me after getting into trouble with the police, so I moved to the other side of the country. Fishing's better here an all.'

'Newport no good then?' I ask making conversation as we head for the front door.

'Docks were alright, whiting, pouting, eels and flounder, I had a good bass there once.' He grabs the door handle, 'and at Tredegar house the tench were awesome, have you ever caught a tench son?'

And that's where it hits me, it's like being struck by lightning, for a moment I think my heads going to burst.

'Blimey son are you alright? You look awful.' He says as I drop back against the wall. 'Are you having some kind of seizure?'

'You're alright Paul,' I gasp, 'I get sudden migraines,' I lie effortlessly, I've got some pills in the car.'

'Let me get 'em for you son, you look bloody dreadful.' He says, 'it must have been that stuff you moved I told you it were heavy.'

'I'm fine mate don't worry,' I straighten up and carefully open the door. 'I'll be okay.'

I stagger down the path and fall into my car. I open the dashboard and remove a fruit pastel from its bag and palm it into my mouth. After thirty seconds I turn back to Paul, anxiously waiting by his door and give him a thumbs up and a smile then start the car and drive away but as soon as I'm out of sight I pull over into a dark lay by and turn off the engine.

My head feels like it is going to explode, I'm reeling and before I go any further I need to explain.

Amnesia is weird, it's happened, I've come to and I've got amnesia, I can't remember a thing.

I go outside there are two cars parked outside the building. The one on the right is a Vauxhall Astra, the car next to it is a mini but it's not the proper mini, not the original one. It's the remake, bigger, not as elegant.

Behind the cars are bushes and these are buddleia.

So I can't remember anything but I can go outside and give you the names of all the things around me. I can remember what the buddleia is called and I can remember the smell of its flowers even though they're too far away from me to know whether or not they have a scent.

Amnesia didn't take the world away from me, I can still remember what it's all called and how it all goes together, what I've lost, what was stolen from me, is my place in it, who I am and what I've done is gone.

But then, every now and again something happens, something now touches on something then. I didn't tell you (it's in the other blog) that before I went to Cardiff Will and I were invited to a party, it was a thank you for some work we've done. Trish, one of the girls there was *very* drunk and she kissed me. So I'm holding her and kissing her (it s seconds honest, well maybe a minute) and I just know that I've done this before. Trish is not quite the right height and she doesn't taste quite right but I've been here before, this isn't a new experience.

Then remember Stan's bike, the second I'm on it and riding it, it's all familiar somehow. Both of these are like a gentle nudge, what happened in Paul's hall was like a hammer blow.

'Have you ever caught a tench son? That's what he said and there and then I'm stood beside a lake holding a landing net. The guy beside me is struggling, the rod's bent over and the drag of the reel is screaming. My heart is pounding, honestly it's like a drum.

All around anglers come running to see, men and boys, this pond is usually just small fish roach, skimmers and eels, rarely anything bigger.

I put the net in the water, I'm not sure what to do.

'I'll bring it to you, just keep the net still, then lift when he's inside.' The guy beside me tells me as he pulls the fish to the surface.

It's a huge tench, a monster, everyone gasps around me leaning forward and craning their necks to see. It's on the surface thrashing and splashing as the guy steers it towards the net and then into it. I lift it smoothly, feeling the fishes weight as I swing the net carefully around and lower it slowly down onto the bank.

All the other kids are patting me on the back as the guy reaches into the net and lifts it out.

It is the most awesome creature, bottle green on the sides, orange yellow underneath. Its fins are black, its tail is like those big wide brushes that you paint walls with and its eyes are bright glowing red like its got batteries inside its head. We all kneel around it watching the guy unhook it, the hook looks so small against its chubby lips and doesn't even leave a mark as he pulls it out.

He lowers it carefully almost reluctantly back into the water and we all watch the huge fish swim away like nothing's happened. The guy thanks me, patting me on the back and telling me that I'd netted it like an expert.

It's my birthday, I'm eight years old and this is the most exciting thing that's ever happened to me. For the first time in my life I feel properly proud of something that I've done and the man beside me is my dad.

How could I ever forget my dad?

I sit in the car, crying like a baby and raging, part of me wants to kill somebody, part of me just wants to curl up and scream.

I feel elation and I feel rage that I can't articulate, there was no children's home no growing up as a loner, there was family, my family. My dad used to take me fishing and we caught tench. On a lake surrounded by trees, there were lilies on the water and an old boat house, dad parked across the field and we'd carry our gear to the lake chatting about what we might catch.

We were a team, how could I forget my dad?

It's an hour before I can drive, I've just got too many thoughts in my head. Should I go around to see Adam, beat the truth out of him if necessary or should I hold onto the cards that I've got.

There's a sort of calm logic that kicks in sometimes, it stops me from charging in and enables me to step back and look at things calmly.

The important thing for now is that I know. As I drive back along a much quieter motorway the thing I feel more than anything else (apart from a raging headache) is relief. It's like a dam bursting, the rest is going to come now, I'm sure of this, I'm positive. For the time being I'll keep these cards close to my chest until I know exactly what I'm dealing with. But despite my sincere resolve, when I get back home in the early hours of the morning, my hands are still shaking.

I lie in my bed completely exhausted but I can't sleep my
brain is racing, what's left of the night crawls past and
eventually I slide into sleep.
Barely an hour later the angry buzz of my alarm wakes me
with a start, I stab the snooze button and shatter the clock
into a hundred pieces. That's the seventh clock that I've
broken, as I said before if you have augmented strength the
world around you suddenly becomes very fragile.
I lie quietly for a moment, all the different thoughts and
ideas that had been racing around my mind have evaporated
and only one remains. You remember what I said about the
calm logic? I know in my heart, without a shadow of a doubt
that the road that opened up before me last night with the
tench will lead me ultimately to the monster in the corridor,
the scarlet man. This is my journey now, my quest if you like
but its something that's going to happen, I've got no control.
It's like I'm on a train, I must allow it to complete its journey
before I can act.

I'm in work on the dot and Wil is in a flap, it turns out that
the reason I was sent to Oxford was so that I could do the
talk about computer security to the chamber of Trade and
commerce but –
'The dag blasted police Commissioner is going to be there

and he wants to see me afterwards,' Wil blusters throwing up his hands.

'Blimey mate what have you done?' I giggle.

He laughs despite his mood. 'Stephen my dear boy, I'll have you know that I am and always have been, an upright and above board sort of fellow. Upholding the law and being obedient to it always and in all . . . uh circumstances.'

'What about Bob's stag night,' Helen shouts from the corner. 'You're still banned from the hotel six years later.'

'What's this?' I laugh as Wil blushes scarlet.

'The reception ended with a raid by the Bomb squad and the Fire brigade had to get Wil and the stripper down off the roof.' Helen collapses into hysterics as Wil impersonates a windmill with his arms.

'You took a stripper to a wedding reception?'

'No, no of course not,' Wil blusters, 'I'm not dense dear boy, no it was nothing like that, I was the best man, I organised the stripper.'

'You organised a stripper for your mate's wedding reception?' I gasp, laughing myself as the whole office collapses in hysterics around us.

'No of course not,' Wil protests, 'Stephen don't be dense, I'm not going to organise a stripper for a wedding reception am I? What kind of man do you think I am, no, I organised the stripper for the stag night but I got the dates mixed up and gave her the wrong one.'

I'm laughing too much to reply, the headache I've had since last night is suddenly long gone.

'Look,' Wil throws up both arms in a desperate attempt to still the hilarity, 'I need to leave in ten minutes and it would be really . . . ah beneficial if I gave at the very least the appearance of knowing what I'm talking about . . .'

'What are they asking you about?' I manage, still chuckling.

'Phishing Stephen, not fishing, phishing.' Will answers quickly.

For a moment I'm back beside the lake holding the landing net. 'Okay broadly speaking there's three different types.'

Wil grins, 'names and illustrations please.'

'Okay, well firstly there's bulk fishing.'

'An illustration please.'

'The American fleet is in the pacific, the officers are away, the crew are lazing about on deck. The cook complains he has nothing fresh for lunch, one of the sailors chucks a hand grenade overboard the explosion stuns a couple of dozen skipjack . . .'

'Skipjack?'

'Tuna mate, they all float up to the surface and the crew can just net them out.'

'So bulk phishing is like fishing with explosives,' Wil nods enthusiastically.

'Yes mate, completely indiscriminate, send thousands of emails out, anyone daft enough to click on the link you can harvest their data.'

'Right, next one.'

'Spear phishing.' I tell him.

'Where you dive in the water and target a specific fish?'

'Yes Wil, you find out as much as you can about the target, what their interests are, what Facebook groups they belong to. That way you can target them with an email that they're much more likely to fall for.'

'And the third?'

'The third is Whaling.'

'Oh bloody hell Stephen, wasn't phishing bad enough.'

'Whaling is where you target the boss, the CEO, the head of the organisation.'

Wil nods, 'okay everyone,' he turns to the rest of the office. 'I need a slogan.

'If in doubt don't click.' I suggest.

'Not catchy enough, needs to rhyme.' Wil waves his arms dismissively.

'I know,' Karen the typist sticks up her hand. 'Think before you click and you won't be a . . .'

'Yes thank you Karen, anyone else?'

'If you don't want to fail then check all of your mail.' Helen suggests after a moment.

Wil looks at her for a long moment.

'If in doubt don't click,' he says turning back to me then he saunters out of the office.

'Helen I'm popping down to the citizen's centre, just check that the code has bedded in alright.

Helen nods and I follow Wil out of the office.

I'm in the citizens centre in minutes, it's a bomb site, there's papers all over the floor, a desk on its side and Janie kneeling beside Beryl (one of her volunteers) both women are clearly startled and upset.

'Did you see them?' Janie gasps as I walk in, they left seconds ago, please tell me you still have *his* phone number.'

'I don't, what did they look like?' I gasp dropping beside the two.

'Tall, two peas in a pod, dark suits brown overcoats.'

I'm on my feet bolting for the door, 'ring the police, I'll see if I can follow them and get a reg number.'

I'm furious, fuming, they're okay just shaken up but when I get my hands on those two . . . it's then it occurs to me that I don't have my costume.

I look up and down the street outside, there's no sign, I hurry to Harry's on the corner, it's a joke come novelty shop, he's got a load of party masks on a stand just inside the door. Harry's got his back to me behind the counter, I grab a large clown mask and put it on as I head to the counter.

'Hey Harry,' I shout putting on an Irish accent (it's the only one I can do) 'How does this look?'

'It looks like £7.99 to me,' Harry replies squinting up at me through his cracked bifocals.

'Keep the change,' I tell him hurrying from the shop after I've flung him a tenner.

This is the poor side of town so (thankfully) there's no CCTV, there's not many people about and no sign of the two that Janie described but there's still a chance.

If they came by car then there's no access to this street, they'd have to park behind the pub and then walk around the mini mart and then up the street to the citizens centre.

I run to the wall opposite and scramble up it, then onto and along the garage roof.

The site of a man in a clown mask doing parkour is only of passing interest to those on the street below.

I run along the roofs and leap off the end landing in a back garden where a girl in a striped bikini is lying on a towel sunbathing.

'Lovely day for it,' I shout to her through the mask as I run along the side of her house and into her front garden.

There across the road is the car park, there's a black BMW with its engine running and two guys in brown coats walking casually towards it like they've got all day.

Showtime!

As they open the back doors and start to get in, I arrive

directly at the front of the vehicle. I reach under the front bumper with both hands and then lift the car up over my head, then I step back and let it drop.

It crashes into the concrete, stalling the engine and sending the driver flying forward into the exploding airbag.

The guy behind him on the right was half way into the car, the impact sends him flying and because his feet are still inside the car there's no way that he can break the impact and he slams his head face first into the concrete.

This wasn't what I had intended, there's blood everywhere he's clearly done himself some serious damage. I leap over the roof for the guy on the drivers left, he's on his knees but he landed better, he's drawing a handgun.

I wallop him a couple of times as hard as I dare then put him out with a slap.

The driver's out of the car, on his hands and knees, he looks terrified, I stomp around to him. 'Who sent you?'

'Barclay, Alan Barclay that's all I know I swear.'

He's only a kid, he doesn't look old enough to drive and he's absolutely terrified, 'run.'

'What?'

'I'll give you a head start.'

He's on his feet in a second and running for his life.

There's nobody I can see, I race up the side of the garage onto the roof pulling my phone from my pocket.

I pull off the mask and jam it under a loose tile.

'I need an ambulance to the car park at the bottom of tunnel terrace, two men one unconscious, the other bleeding badly, you better send the police as well.' I tell the operator, 'it was the masked guy, there's a gun here on the floor as well.'

I'm back beside the guy who's really hurt, he seems to be fitting now, blimey what if I've killed him?
The operator is more anxious about the gun than the guy telling me to stay with it and not too touch it.

The police in all fairness are there in three minutes.
'God what happened to him?' The first copper (Andrew he tells me) says hurrying to the guy I'm kneeling beside.
'There's a gun by there,' I point to the gun. The second copper (Malcolm it turns out) picks up the gun with a pen and drops it into a clear bag, then he goes to check on the unconscious guy.
'I went into the citizens centre to check their computer, the two girls were on the floor they'd been roughed up and the place had been smashed up.'
Andrew nods listening intently, as he checks the guy over.
'The girls said the guys that did it had just left and were wearing dark suits and raincoats.'
'So you went looking for them sir?' Andrew starts checking the guy's pockets.
'I knew if they'd come by car here was the closest place to

park. I thought I might be able to get their reg number.

'That was smart thinking sir.'

'It's Stephen.'

'Well Stephen we usually advise that you leave the crime fighting to the professionals.' Andrew uses his own pen to remove a gun from inside his own jacket.

I laugh, 'I wasn't gonna fight them mate, I just figured I might be able to get their reg number.'

Andrew nods looking suitably impressed.

Then soon as I comes round the corner I heard a bang, like a car crash and a lot of shouting.'

'Did you see anything sir?'

'This is going to sound stupid.'

'Don't you worry about that sir, 'Malcolm comes and drops on his haunches beside us. 'Just tell us what you saw.'

'Well somebody jumped over that roof,' I point to the roof opposite. 'The sun was in front of them so I couldn't see colour or detail but there was definitely someone up there running away.'

Both PC's look at each other knowingly.

'I've seen him before.'

'Where and when,' Andrew asks me but he doesn't look convinced.

'Aye I got hauled in by two of your officers about it, James and Hooper was it?'

Both PC's smirk.

'I fixed his laptop, he just walked into our office with it one night.'

'Your kidding?' Andrew's impressed now, 'Aye I nearly jumped out of my skin, I thought it was the cleaner and I turned round and there's this dude in a Halloween costume.' Andrew laughs whilst Malcolm gets back on the radio wanting to know why the ambulance was taking so long (or words to that effect.)

It turns out that all the ambulances are tied up, we have a (frankly ludicrous) system in this country that ambulance crews have to stay with their vehicle when they take a patient in to hospital, they have to wait until the patient can be unloaded and taken in. Because the government decided to cut the number of hospital beds some years ago, there is now, nowhere near enough beds. This means that crews often have to spend the whole of their shift just sat waiting outside hospitals.

More to the point it can often mean that you can't get an ambulance when you need one.

Which means the police are going to have to take them in in their patrol car.

Despite the fact that the very first piece of advise that's given with accident victims is don't move them. Officers Andrew and Malcolm grab an arm each and I grab his feet, we carry him gingerly over to the police car and fold him into a sitting position on the back seat.

He looks bloody awful, I'm sure I've killed him, I honestly don't think that I've ever seen so much blood.

Then as Andrew buckles him up, Malcolm and I go and grab the other fella.

'We'll take them in, look we'll need a statement.' Malcolm tells me as we head back to the patrol car.

'I'm in the office all day tomorrow I'll give you my card.'

'That will be fine, do you mind checking on the girls in the citizen centre. They should be looked at really.'

'I was going there anyway, soon as we're done here. I'll drive them over to the hospital if necessary.'

Malcolm shakes my hand and they're off.

Soon as they're gone, it's as silent as a grave again. There's not a soul about, I can hear the hustle and bustle of the mini mart, a train somewhere to my right and the low murmur of traffic behind. The place is a grimy oasis of calm in the busy noisy city, my eyes fall on the dark stain over the concrete, I turn and head for the citizens centre.

The Dinner party – Chapter nine.

By eight o'clock that evening I've recovered the clown mask and destroyed it and I'm now in the posh part of the city, not my usual neck of the woods at all.

I'm on the rooftop of an old Victorian factory that's been converted into luxury flats looking down at a huge detached three storey with swimming pool and squash courts.

They're obviously having a dinner party tonight which I hadn't banked upon but that isn't going to stop me.

The great and the good file up the drive after each of them is deposited at the gate. I don't know how many of them are dirty but its dirty money that's paying for this party and that's good enough for me.

What was it that Emma had said about working around the edge?

I'm in the grounds in a minute; there are a few guys in suits in the grounds and at least two German Shepherds.

I'm up the back corner of the house and in through a guest bedroom window. It takes me five minutes to find what I'm looking for and it's even better than I hoped.

Eleven minutes and it's done.

I stand silently in the room, I have two options now. I hear laughter from one of the rooms below, raucous laughter, a room full of laughing people, it makes up my mind for me.

I'm out of the room and along the landing. The green bandaged skull makes me jump as it appears in a dressing table mirror seen through an open bedroom door then there's a guy standing guard at the top of the stairs.
I slap him across the head and catch him as he falls, I look at the layout of the rooms on the floor below. I hate the thought of having to kill a dog but now I can see where the room is I realise that with a bit of luck I won't have to.
I reach into my pocket and pull out what looks like a small gauze pad, I stopped using it cos it was scaring me let alone everybody else. It's more of Adam's military tec, think of it as a broken speaker, it'll boost the bass and amplify your voice he told me and he was right, with it I sound like Death! I push it up under the front of my mask.

I hesitate outside the closed double doors, listening to the bustle of the room.
This is risky and it is unwise, then I see Janie and Beryl huddled together on the floor and I kick the doors down.
I spent five hours sat with them in casualty before they were sent home with tablets.
'Alan Barclay,' my voice booms out like a judge pronouncing

doom.

There's instant pandemonium, screaming women leap and fall backwards from the table, falling over each other. Three men at least are reaching into their jackets whilst another four charge me.

But to me everything's happening in slow motion and everybody is in everybody else's way.

The first two reach me hands clawing for my face, I bang their heads together, the noise of the collision setting my teeth on edge.

The next one runs into my elbow as I grab the fourth by the collar and belt, lift him over my head and hurl him through the plate glass window, as I suspected a second later there is a loud splash.

I turn for the nearest that reached into his jacket, he's got a handgun that he's raising to fire. I grab a fallen chair and slam it into his wrist, the gun goes off shooting him in the foot. Two more with guns but there's chaos in the room, people screaming, desperately trying to get out falling over each other.

The first gunman lunges forward trying to get a better position but he's overdone it, he's too close, I grab his hand crushing his fingers onto the gun then I lift him bodily and hurl him into the other gunman whose own gun goes off shattering part of the chandelier.

'You send thugs to beat up old ladies,' the voice is awful

really, I hate it but have to admit it's effective. Two more guys leap at me from either side, one clawing at my mask the other punching me manically in the neck. I bang their heads together setting my teeth on edge again.

'Two elderly volunteers giving up their time trying to help (Janie would murder me if she knew I called her elderly) and what? You set your boys on them!'

Alan Barclay's against the wall now, he's early forties, smartly dressed, his suit probably cost more than most people earn in a year. He's white with fright, his lips are moving but no sound is coming out.

There's a woman on me now, smart, posh dress, she stabs me in the eye with a fork, screaming and pressing it in as hard as she can. sharpfilm is military tec however, she's not even going to scratch it but she doesn't know that. I thrust her aside, she keeps her footing but awkwardly, staggering backwards, then with a crack her heel and ankle break together dropping her screaming to the floor.

With a roar half a dozen suited thugs burst into the room, they'd been trying to get in but were prevented by all of those who were dashing out.

'Kill him, kill him, finish him!' Alan Barclay finds his voice, the first German Shepherd (or is it Alsatian, I'm never sure) leaps at me whilst the second (rather wonderfully) sinks his teeth into the backside of one of the thugs I'd knocked to the floor who's trying to get back up.

Now if you think about it dogs have got one big disadvantage, sure a dog bite is painful (and frequently gets infected) but at the end of the day that's all that they've got. No claws like a big cat just teeth. I catch Fido by the muzzle with both hands, closing his mouth and keeping it shut with one hand whilst I get the other under his stomach, lift him and lob him out of the window.

Yes he'll be straight out of the pool but what's he going to do then? He can't get back in the house because someone's locked all of the down stair doors!

Back in the room its carnage, a huge guy, grabs me in a bear hug as two more rush forward straight at me. I lean back against the big guy and kick out with both feet at the two on comers, catching both in the throat and dropping them gagging to the floor. Then I plant my feet into the ground and haul the big fella up and over my shoulder and hurl him across the room. He lands heavily on the woman with the broken ankle who's still grasping the fork.

There's more coming into the room now, all clueless, charging forward, getting in each other's way, stumbling over bodies on the floor. All convinced they can win with force of numbers. I dance between them slapping and punching, it's all so gloriously unfair. They're toddlers in slow motion, I'm cheating, a professional footballer in a primary school five aside game.

But they're thugs, they're bullies, this is where the tables are turned, this is where they see what it's like on the other side. There are sirens outside now, police and ambulances, funny how they can find so many, so quickly, when it's the posh side of town.

The police however are waiting for the firearms unit and I've got Alan all to myself.

The room looks like a news report from a warzone, I slide Alan up the wall by his throat.

'You sent thugs against two elderly women tell me why?'

My voice is like death, it's completely surreal, it's like I'm watching somebody else, listening to somebody else.

Alan doesn't have an answer, he looks like a terrified child, I almost feel sorry for him.

I punch him as hard as I dare in the stomach then grab his ear, squeezing and twisting without pity.

'You close down operations tonight, you stop what you're doing, you get *one* warning and that was it. I'm the yellow card son, you continue with what you're doing and next time I'm red.

I lay hands on him, hoist him over my head and hurl him out of the broken window, his leg hits the diving board with a crack as his body lands in the water.

I'm out of the house and out of the grounds before the police armed response team are in through the front door.

In a minute I'm back on the roof of the flats, there's a huge crowd of outraged and terrified party goers outside the house with the police and ambulance crews. I heat the same phrase over and over again.

Law abiding citizens.

In the crowd, from my vantage point, I can see several famous faces. Local Council bosses, staff from the MP's office, luminaries from the Chamber of trade and commerce.

I pick up the tablet I've left on the roof.

Another one of Adam's toys, the military use them all the time, so theirs are robust and durable. I read the reply to the email that I sent and smile under my mask.

Word of advice here, if you have any sensitive material on your computer, don't ever let a hacker into your home and leave them unattended.
I've just beaten up a rising underworld star in front of his friends and colleagues and it was all of it totally unnecessary.
I didn't need to do it, at least in the sense of getting a result.

The eleven minutes I spent on his computer will have finished him far more completely than a kicking in a dinner party. The people screaming about a law abiding citizen tonight will be hastily denying that they ever knew him tomorrow.

One of the people I really wanted to meet at Oxford was Crystal known online as NumbersAngel. Crystal is that utterly wonderful (and exceptionally useful) combination of genius hacker and qualified accountant.

Whilst I was bouncing Alan and his friends around his dining room, Crystal was sending full copies of all of his accounts to the National Press.

According to Crystal, Alan has been a very bad lad he's using several small legit companies to hide the activities of an equal number of extremely dubious one's based primarily around drugs and prostitution.

I told Crystal I was sure the guy was dirty so I parked outside his house trying to access his Wifi. Next thing I know this dude in a mask turns up and starts beating everybody up, so I sneaked in and emailed her from one of his computers whilst everyone was distracted. Crystal's always online, so it was easy to get hold of her and as I'm on his computer it's easy to give her access, then once she's got access there's nowhere to hide.

Following morning Wil is in fine form, he's giving us in the office a blow by blow account of how he had all in the meeting eating out of his hands with his tales of sailors and hand grenades.

I laugh with everyone else, only Wil could turn a five minute briefing into a four hour monologue.

'So what did the Police Commissioner want?' I ask when he finally stops for air.

'Ah yes well uh . . . it's a tad awkward actually.'

'Go on,' Helen and I say in unison.

'Well it was about our costumed friend.'

'The one that Hendrick's Computer Services is proud to stand alongside.' Helen asks dryly.

'Well ah . . . I don't recall that is I don't think that those were my exact . . . um actual . . .'

'Proud to stand alongside.' Helen reminds him, turning to me for support.

'Your exact words mate . . . in fact don't the two of you share the same chair on occasion?' I agree.

'Ah now . . . yes about that . . . well you see it ah . . . might be good if we distance ourselves from uh . . .'

'Wil?' Helen narrows her eyes and Wil squirms.

'Look I'm really sorry and yes I'm glad we could help . . . but this was ah . . . before the um Commissioner and I had out little chat last . . . um Yesterday. He was furious, he was tamping and that was before the punch up at the dinner he was taking his wife to last night.'

'The police Commissioner was at Alan Barclay's party?' I blurt.

Blimey I hope it wasn't his wife with the fork.

'A law abiding citizen by all accounts, gives money to charity and everything.' Wil retorts.

'Wil the news this morning said there was gunfire and the police recovered over a dozen firearms from the scene. Now Any-Man doesn't use a gun so if its' a law abiding party where did all the guns come from?' Helen asks Wil pointedly.

'More to the point,' Elsie one of our freelancers looks up from her keyboard. 'Both of the main News channels have extended their lunchtime programmes. The one citing shock revelations about a local business man, unnamed but they're linking it directly to the attack last night.'

'Well that's not going to be Alan Barclay is it?' Wil scoffs throwing up both arms. 'I've met the man, charming absolutely erm salt of the ah community, a nicer more decent chap you couldn't hope to . . erm . . . damn it Elsie we're in the same club!'

'The same club,' Helen scoffs, 'oh well that's sacrosanct then, all the guns must have been at the party for wholesome reasons only. Maybe they wanted to take pot shots at the

171

meringue or maybe they have a rat problem.'

Wil smirks along with the rest of us, 'look I can assure all of you, I can put your minds at rest, Alan Barclay is straight up as good as they come, as honest as the day is ah long. He'll shake you firmly by the hand and look you in the eye. I'm a good erm even excellent judge of character. Alan's with the angels but the Vigilante what do we know about him? Where he goes and what he does.'

'Well we know where he was yesterday.' Helen says.

'We know where he was yesterday evening,' Wil corrects.

'We know where he was yesterday morning too, he was beating up the thugs who ruffed up Janie and one of her volunteers, Steve saw him.'

Wil's face falls in horror, 'was Janie alright? What on earth happened?' He asks quickly staring wildly at me in alarm.

I tell him pretty much the same story I told the police.

'Stephen m'boy, why didn't you tell me as soon as I got in I've been stood here gassing like . . .'

'Couldn't get a word in edgeways mate,' I tell him with a grin.

'You're sure they're alright?'

'Wil soon as I'd finished with the police I went back over there and drove them to casualty. They were both shaken up but no real harm.'

'What about the office?'

'A bombsite Will, they'd kicked in the side of the computer box, smashed up the monitor and ripped all the cables out of everything. Obviously I didn't have chance to try any of the equipment.'

Wil nods thoughtfully. 'I'm betting you can guess my next question.'

'Was Alan Barclays name on the list?'

Wil nods.

'Sorry mate, it was one of the first up.'

Wil stands stock still, thinking hard for a few moments.

'Okay then, Helen . . .'

'I've already got all the hardware they'll need in the boot of my car, I just need you to sign it off.' Helen tells him handing him an A4 sheet.

Wil grins as he signs it.

'I'll go along with her and reinstall the database again.'

'No Helen you go and do your bit, I'll send Steve along later.' He points to his office and mouths, *we need to talk.*

I drop into the chair in Wil's office, he has a swivel master deluxe in here as well behind his desk, I've got a swivel master standard which is a little too low and squeaks. Wil doesn't use his office much preferring to sit with the chaps (although I'm the only other fella in the office.) The office is only for confidential high level stuff so I know something is up.

'Is this about the costumed guy?' I ask as Wil sits down and leans across his desk.

'Operation mousetrap,' Wil whispers.

'You cannot be serious,' I hiss back.

'You my friend have been tasked with the job of tracking him down.' Wil tells me quietly, with the air of one bestowing the greatest privilege.

'The police want *me* to find him?' I gasp.

'The police have asked me to put my best man on it, that's you old boy!'

'Wil I . . .'

'They're paying a fortune; seriously for once they've got money to burn.'

'Wil I'm a programmer, I'm not a detective, I wouldn't have a clue where to . . .'

'It's all decided, we've worked it all out.'

'Oh god.'

'Social media.'

'Wil I loathe social media, I don't have a facebook page, I'm not on twitter . . .'

'But you know how it works.'

'Wil so does most of the population.'

'Look the Commissioner and his wife and me . . .'

'Oh lord.'

'Think we've found his Achilles heel,' Wil pauses for

dramatic effect. 'Publicity!'

'Publicity?'

'The costume, the mask, well it's all just an ego trip isn't it, why else would a grown man be doing this.'

I stare quietly at Wil aiming for an inscrutable expression.

'Yeah, well what about you posh boy?'

'I'm sorry m'boy I don't understand . . ?'

'You make a great thing about being honest and above board when you're far from either.

'Stephen I . . .'

'You have two sets of prices, double standards in any language. Banks and all those companies with money get charged the one, charities and voluntary groups you charge the other. You over charge all of those who can well afford it in order to subsidise those who can't. You're Robin Hood mate and me and your staff love you for it and are proud to work for you.'

Wil looks shell shocked and starts to tear up.

'The point is mate you do this cos that's who you are, everything's broken so you go out of your way to fix what you can. It's not about ego or publicity, you're a good guy and good does what it is. What if the costumed guy is the same, he can see that everything's broken and he's just trying to fix what he can?'

Wil can't speak for his moments then needs a handkerchief to remove something from his eye.

'He has many pages on facebook,' Wil says quietly without looking me in the eye, 'and eh that sparrow thing.'

'Twitter?'

'That's the fella, could you just ah . . . work through them . . . see which might be genuine and which obviously aren't and then erm . . . that was most kind of you to . . . what you said I'll . . . that I do . . .'

I rise from my chair with a smile, 'I'll put a folder together for you by the end of the week.'

'That would be super and erm . . . thank you Stephen.'

I loathe social media, you're on there no time before you get into an argument, you explain your point of view and promptly get abuse or dismissed with *fake news*.

You can dismiss anything with the phrase fake news, public services are stretched to breaking point no they're not that's fake news.

There is *real* poverty and suffering in one of the richest countries in the world. No there isn't, that's fake news.

The world is not flat its round, we can prove this by flying planes around it and looking at it from space. No the world is flat and all evidence to the contrary is, all of it, fake news.

I spend the rest of the day looking at my alter ego's activity on line.

There are a dozen pages and accounts for Any-Man and over thirty for the Vigilante.

It's a bit of an eye opener actually, several of the pages look really professional, two are even selling merchandise!

You can buy replica masks (not replicas at all I hasten to add) and tasteful red V badges.

The V incidentally was for victory originally, the colours of a motorcycle racing team (that went a whole season without winning anything.) The leathers were replicas of the team colours, cos the team had members in the TA Adam bought the job lot when they disbanded.

The replica masks are just Halloween skulls sprayed green nothing like my far more professional tastefully designed construct.

One of the pages also boast numerous rooftop views of the city at night, allegedly taken by me whilst I'm on duty (whatever that means.)

The caption makes it clear that only a superhero could access these views but the truth is they've all clearly been taken by a drone in daylight and then filtered.

There's several diaries, on some of the pages with mission statements and the like. *I walk the line between good and evil* you know the kind of thing.

It's all rather amusing rather than flattering but if I'm honest it's pretty obvious that all of it is fiction. They may look authentic to begin with but as soon as you delve deeper it doesn't take a genius to realise that they're wannabe's rather than the real thing. If this isn't apparent from the content then it soon is when you look at the comments or more specifically the replies to the comments.

There's one exception, which is basically just photos of the places where confrontations occurred and a list of every incident.

The list is authentic and an eye opener, when you see them all written down you suddenly start to realise just how many there are of them.

In addition to the list there's all the pictures, it's like they've been following me around.

There's a photo of the bloodstain on the concrete in the car park at Tunnel Terrace and there are photos of Alan Barclay's house, inside and out, broken windows, bloodstains on the floorboards and a broken diving board. This last lot were posted an hour ago, how on earth could they get inside his house?

More to the point how have they compiled the list?

Did they ring around the hospitals? If so would NHS staff give out names and details about injuries? I'm certain that they won't, equally I'm certain that the list is by and large accurate.

The information must have come from the inside but who

and where?

I put together a folder full of screenshots and information dumps, putting the best one's near the front. Then I hack the sites and see what I can glean from the code.

One of the guy that's selling the stuff says that all profits are going to charity but his code says otherwise, I send some screenshots and bank account details to the charity commission.

Now my time is my own for a day or so and the first thing I do is look up Sandra Dobson who's still at Oxford university.

Sandra it soon transpires likes her Social media as she's on everything but it's all about her rather than her work.

I try a phone call first, she answers with her name and a posh accent.

'Sandra hi,' I reply, trying for calm and professional. 'You don't know me, my name is Stephen Bishop and I'm trying to find out some information about the codex de Estelle.'

She hangs up without another word.

I get onto her work site, she's a biologist so I know where to look.

It takes me a little while to hack into her department's server but once in I soon find a dozen or so hidden files. There's nothing on the codex but she has been playing fast and loose with the departmental budget.

In essence most of the funding comes from annual grants, if all of the money hasn't been spent by the April of each year the value of the remaining money is deducted from the following years grant.

You see the same thing with local councils who are always busy repairing roads and services in March making sure they're using up all of the allotted money for that year. To ensure they get the full amount for the next financial year. Sandra's basically moved any money around rather than spending it and when it is eventually spent it's all on the department. There's no personal gain in this but it's still fraud or from my point of view leverage.

Estelle Parr – Chapter ten.

The next day I'm not expected in work because I'm supposed to be going through Any-Man's online activities. Because I've already done this I'm free to drive down to Oxford again.

Sandra is a creature of habit, lunch at 1pm in *The Violet garden* a large and sprawling cafe opposite her lab. She's easy to spot, carrying coffee and sandwiches as well as a pile of folders.

I wait until she's settled at a single table at the very back. I walk up to her and place my hand on the back of the chair opposite.

'Is this seat taken?' I enquire politely.

'Yes, I'm expecting guests and there's plenty of other empty tables around.' She replies acidly.

I pull out the chair and drop into it. 'You dine alone Sandra, you make a point of it.'

She glances up at me furiously, then turns to look for one of the staff.

'You can call somebody if you like but if you do I'll email Tom Hillard at Alansbrooke investments and tell him what you do with all of the unspent finance. I've got full copies of the contents of the folder you've named Kingstone.'

That does it, I have her full attention now and she's livid. 'So you're a dirty little hacker out to blackmail . . .'

'Hacker yes, blackmail no, its leverage, the only way I can get you to answer a simple question.'

'What question?'

'It was only two days ago, how often do you hang up on people?'

Realisation dawns.

'How did you get into those files? We've got excellent state of the art . . .'

'You've got basic cyber security and you leave trails. Tell me what I want to know and I'll tell you how to beef up your security without spending a pound.'

'I haven't profited . . .'

'I know that but it's still fraud which makes it leverage for me, if you'd just answered the question in the first place.'

'Who sent you?'

'I'm a hacker who's acting on his own, I've found something that I don't understand and I want answers.'

'Where did you get my name?' She's powerless and she knows it and she doesn't like it. Her hands are trembling but its anger rather than fear.

'I'm not answering your questions until you start answering mine. The codex de Estelle, what is it?'

She stares at me silently, angrily for a full minute until –

'I'm not going away Sandra and I will . . .'

'Wild medicine, have you heard of it?'

'In the context I think you mean it's the belief that the cure for all maladies exist in nature and often under our noses, like Dock leaves growing next to nettles.'

'So the hacker has a brain?'

'How do you think we do what we do?'

'Botanical medicine goes back to the Neanderthals, that's 40,000 years ago. We've discovered the remains of medicinal plants in a cave in Northern Spain, they were in the remains of a Neanderthal's dental calculus. Throughout history there is a trail of records and studies, Al-Beruni and Avicenna started cataloguing them a thousand years ago in the middle –East. They were referenced and copied by more generations of scientists century after century.'

She stops for a long sip of coffee. 'Nowadays a quarter of our medicines are based on plants and many of the discoveries were made hundreds of years ago. Estelle Parr was a woman out of her time, a truly brilliant intellect in a time of male dominated Academia but as well as brains Estelle had the looks to turn the head of kings and she soon acquired resources to match. A fortune, a king's ransom was hers so she used it. She set about compiling a directory of all the knowledge of a world's worth of plant and fungus based medicine and research. Estelle believed that every species had something, maybe a cure, maybe a poison. It would be her life's work to discover everything that could be discovered and to catalogue it all for future generations. She seemed to know instinctively that science would progress and advance, her aim was to provide science with the ultimate reference book that her name might live forever.' She takes another sip of coffee. 'Estelle was right, nowadays genetic sequencing is leading the way, it's feasible to sequence the genes of pretty much anything. Biochemists are using DNA encoded chemical libraries, they use the DNA to select and synthesize compounds that attach to targets like enzymes and receptors. Compounds are labelled with short DNA fragments that act as barcodes. To identify those that bind successfully, researchers read the combined DNA sequence. This DNA barcode information is vital for us to progress in plant-based treatments.'

'So why the secrecy?'

'Because it wasn't just cures and poisons that she discovered.'

'Go on.'

'How did you get my name?'

'You left your business card with the man who found the index at Tredegar house, he's harmless and no threat to you. He only told me because I spent time with him. Go on.'

'You've heard of Alchemy?'

'Album by Dire straits and the process of turning lead into gold.'

'That's the most common supposed application but it is

more the process of turning one thing into another.'

'So looking to turn plants into?'

She looks at me like a Mother looking at a child who's just vomited down his front in polite company. 'Not changing the plant you dolt, using certain chemicals from certain plants to engineer specific changes.'

'What sort of changes?'

'What type would you like? What can you afford?'

'Go on.'

'You've heard of the Viking berserkers?'

I nod.

'Fierce warriors in a trance like state, lethal in battle, if you cut them they barely bleed, they're exceptionally strong and completely ferocious.'

'Henbane?' I reply but I don't know where I've got the word from.

She nods, 'possibly, it was a common weed in Scandinavia at the time, some scholars think it might have been a mushroom Amanita muscaria it's poisonous but it has hallucinogenic properties. If they had found a way to prepare it so it could be ingested. It is said that when the berserkers were in their trance they howled like animals and bit their shields, their faces became red and swollen they would shiver with their teeth chattering and then the rage broke out.'

'So if somebody was looking to make a super-soldier?'

She nods, 'It wouldn't be in this country or the States for that matter, far too many regulations but there are other places where the rules are a little more, shall we say lax.'

I nod slowly.

'So how did you get involved?' She asks quietly, watching me with interest now.

'There's something very odd going on, there are a handful of extremely clever self-contained programs roaming the internet, deleting any reference to the codex. At the same time somebody is searching, primarily public buildings at night . . .'

'Mantis?' She asks with a half smile, 'I watch the news boy and I'm not an idiot.'

Her gaze falls on my left arm (covered by a sleeve) for a second, or maybe I'm just being paranoid.

'The lad that put me on to this is a mate, he's a security guard at the National museum of Wales, she gave him a right kicking, I promised him I'd find out why.'

'What did you say your name was?'

'Stephen Bishop.'

'It's not public buildings that she's interested in Stephen, it's *old* buildings, anything prior to 1945.'

'Go on.'

'Look the codex was a lifetime's work; even with today's advancements the book is full of lost knowledge, old knowledge. The good and the bad and that means that there are all sorts of people who want it and they want it for all sorts of reasons. Look you talked about Super soldiers, the stumbling block with every compound that's known is psychosis, all they give to the body must be measured against the damage they do to the brain but Estelle claimed to have catalogued compounds that overcame this.'

'So what happened to these?'

'Estelle collected together everything that she could, her daughter Maria compiled it but Estelle died before it was finished and Maria found herself alone and in possession of something of great value. Now Maria didn't have her Mother's looks or brains but she was shrewd enough to take advantage of the opportunity. She released the volume as she'd promised her mother but not all of it. The book was split into three sections, cures and medicines, poisons and enhancements then a footnote made it clear that there were additional pages for the second and third sections that she and the publisher had held back as being 'too dangerous for public consumption. These were collected into a codex that would only be available to the *right* people at the right price. Poisons that left no trace and enhancements that bordered on alchemy.'

'So what happened?'

'Well sales of the original volume were far higher than was expected and as the promise of the codex was attracting the attention of some extremely dodgy people Maria gave the codex to her local university. They would examine it at length and make it available to any expert that wanted to study it.'

'And did they?'

'Did they hell, they put it into storage, 'an important scientific work by a woman?' Preposterous! Was the phrase most common at the time apparently but they did however get a copy made and it's this that explains what's been going on. Andersford was a public school with links to the university and a dozen years into the twentieth century four of its senior students were tasked with copying the codex. The copy would be produced in a secure location away from the school and the university and all that is known is that it was a capital within the United Kingdom.

The four youngsters were taken to the un-named city and an upstairs room in an old stone building where each was to produce a copy. They worked through the day and each was thoroughly searched when they left. They were not allowed to take paper or writing implements with them but the boys weren't fools and soon realised that what they were writing down had value. Now the toilet in the building was above the room they were using and from there a window took them out onto the roof. The boys used to sneak out and carve what they were copying down stairs into the bricks of the chimneys.'

'You're kidding?'

She shakes her head. 'It is common to find graffiti on the stones and bricks near roofs. I don't mean modern paint and ink, I mean small carved initials, names and messages from the original builders. Still legible after hundreds of years.'

'Yes, I've seen these for myself.' I tell her, I spend a lot of time on rooftops.

'Well the boys completed their task and returned to their school where they were soon called up for war. Only one of them returned and he no longer had a taste for adventure so the chimney was forgotten, until War loomed again. Two German agents were picked up in London, various ARC wardens had spotted them on rooftops on several occasions and finally had been able to catch them. Eventually after questioning they confessed that it was this that they were looking for, although nobody in Britain knew anything about it. Now Hitler was known to be into the occult so the authorities weren't that concerned assuming that these agents were on a ridiculous wild goose chase. The authorities got a clerical assistant, a dogs body if you like, named Andrew Layton to look into it. Basically he was to visit the sites that the agents had and see if he could find anything. Fortunately young Andrew had a sharp mind. He found nothing at the sites but soon discovered the truth of the codex. The original had been destroyed in a fire when the university burned down in the twenties. He realised that if the copy was out there somewhere then it could be dangerous in the wrong hands but what could he do? They didn't have the man power to search properly. His solution was genius, he went back to his superiors, reported all that he'd discovered and made his suggestion which they loved and put into practice immediately.'

I sigh and smile, 'he went out and carved on chimneys didn't he?'

She smiles back, it's the first time I've seen her smile properly, it suits her. 'London, Cardiff and Edinburgh, every old chimney on every stone building that he could get to. He knew from the agents that it was numbers in sets of three so he just carved whatever came into his head.'

I nod slowly, 'and now there's so many of them there's no way to work out which was the original?'

'And now there's so many of them there's no way we can work out which is the original.' She answers quietly. 'And there's something else isn't there?'

'There is?'

'Not so smart then,' she smirks.

'Go on.'

'Capitals within the UK before the first world war?'

I shake my head.

'Cardiff did not become the capital of Wales until 1955, before that Swansea, Aberystwyth and Caernarfon, all had claims on the title at various times.'

'Mantis is French,' I reply quickly, 'maybe she . . .'

'Is she now! And how would you know that?'

'My mate, he's a big fella, Welsh, he plays a lot of Rugby. He didn't take kindly to getting a kicking from a lass that was half his size but he said the worst of it was she kept firing questions at him in French and he didn't understand a word of it.'

Sandra smiles and takes a bite out of her baguette. 'Estelle divided her time between Kent and Paris, after a spell as the kings mistress she married a Duke. History doesn't tell us which king.'

I sit quietly for a minute watching her eat and wishing I'd ordered something. 'You know you could just photograph all of the chimneys, then use software to read and record everything and bung the lot into a half decent database you could soon . . .'

'What? Work it out? Stephen there's no interest, no will. The original building could have been bombed and destroyed in the war or demolished since or failing that many old chimneys have been removed anyway because we no longer use them. Then what are we doing it for, more poisons? We have enough. Besides a poison that leaves no trace might have been true then but it won't be now. So that just leaves the alchemy, chemical enhancement which will be illegal now so what is the point.'

'So why the cloak and dagger?'

'Because the promise of the codex is a magnet to the very

191

worst type of people, it always has been.'

I sit quietly for a minute thinking hard.

'Would you really have contacted Alansbrooke?'

'Don't be daft,' I tell her with my best smile, 'I just needed a little leverage. Here -' I delve into a pocket and pull out a folded sheet of A5. 'Give this to your IT guy, once it's in you'll just need to restart the computer. He'll see what it is and does, its harmless and you won't be hacked from now on you have my word.' I hand her the sheet, nod, then walk away.

The following day I'm with Wil, the Chief Superintendent and half a dozen suits in the council chambers.

Wil's copied the folder and I'm on power point and in a suit. I don't recognise the Chief Super from the room but he is clearly not a happy man.

'You're saying he's none of them?' He says gruffly, waving the folder at me.

'I'm saying that after a provisional investigation all but three are clearly amateurs trying to make out that they're something that they're not.'

'You can't possibly say that for certain,' a woman with jet black hair and a white lacy dress brandishes the folder. 'You say all of the sites bar the first three are by amateurs but number five has photo's that could only have been taken by somebody on the rooftops.'

'Look at the clock face on page seventeen.' I tell her, getting the image up on the large wall screen. 'It's glossy, reflective and if you look there,' I zoom in. 'You'll see the reflection of the drone that took the photo.' Also the moon is not on either of the wide angles on the same page but given the date and time listed it would have been and there's no cloud. Also look down at the street, there's no shutters over any of the shop windows which there would be at 4AM. These photos are taken by a drone in daylight at 4PM then the photo's run through a filter in photoshop or gimp to make it look like it's taken at night.'

'What about the people selling merchandise?' The chief Super wades in. 'He's obviously getting a cut himself.'

'Possibly, but the guy who says he's putting the proceeds into charity isn't, it's all going straight to his bank. I've sent the details to the charity commission. The other guy selling, well his stuff is so lame . . .'

'What do you mean?' The chief grunts.

'Well the replica mask is just a Halloween skull mask sprayed green.' I point out.

'Exactly like our identikits!'

'Yes,' I concede, 'but I've seen the real thing up close it's far better . . .'

'You've seen him?!' The woman in white gasps.

'Oh yes Silvia,' the Chief snaps, silencing Wil who was just about to answer. 'This chap only went and fixed his laptop for him would you believe?'

'Well why on earth didn't you grab him?' The woman snaps at me.

I stare at her stupidly for a moment, 'I'm sorry how long has he been at large now?' I ask quietly. 'If the police haven't been able to get hold of him what chance have I got?'

'Well you could have tried, you're not exactly small.'

'He is half a foot taller than me and half as big again,' I lie effortlessly, 'I mean how many guys were in that house the other night, armed gangland thugs . . .'

The Chief holds up his hands, 'I'm sure the . . . uh people there were so shocked and Alan Barclay has clearly been taking advantage of the uh . . . good will . . .' The Chief blusters as Wil, behind his back, frantically signals for me to change the subject. '

'Well Alan Barclay seems to have been getting away with murder for months, I was merely saying that if the Vigilante knew he was bad I'm surprised . . . ' Wil looks like he's going to die so I quickly change the subject. 'Sorry the point I was originally making is that if he was involved in the merchandising I'm sure it would be more accurate.'

'You really thing he would care?' A man in a dark suit scoffs, shaking his head.

'You have asked me to do this because the guy is an ego maniac, if that's the case then of course he'll want it right.' I

194

snap back, standing my ground and silencing both of them.

'What about this one on page twenty three?' Another guy in a suit. 'He sounds a right nasty piece of work.'

I flick to his page and smirk, 'look at the comments, hardboy7 tells him that he could take him in a fight, then look how he responds. They're two children arguing in a playground If the *real* Vigilante was that easy to wind up he'd be beating up everyone.'

'But he already . . .'

'I'm sorry no, he's cold and calculated and he's not going to be rowing online with a belligerent eleven year old.' I stand my ground again with the same result.

'The first three then?' The Chief drops his folder onto the table. 'What makes you pick them?'

'Well number three, if I'm honest, I can't quite put my finger on it but there's something that makes it stand out from the others.' I flick through the pages on the power point.

'Number two doesn't say much but every link to the page is encrypted and not just with the routine in house kit. Then we have number one and with that I have a single question, where the hell are they getting all of their information from? Dates, times, locations and injuries, they'd not get that from the hospital surely so where's it all coming from?'

All eyes in the room turn to the Chief.

'Well William you've certainly given us something to think about.' The Chief ignores me and gathers up his folder, then turns to glare silently at me with most of the other suits. I stare back smiling stupidly for a moment wondering what I'm supposed to do, then realisation dawns and I take the hint and leave the room quickly.

Will hurries after me stopping me in the corridor as an elderly lady with a trolley groaning under its burden of sandwiches, cakes, tea and coffee strains past me on her way to the room I've just left. I pinch a sandwich with my best smile to lighten her load.

'Excellent m'boy,' Wil slaps me on the back. 'You must have spent hours . . .'

I shake my head with a mouthful of sandwich.

'Listen Stephen,' he whispers conspiratorially handing me a slip of paper. 'New job,' he looks around quickly, 'Civil Service no less, we're going up in the world.'

'Do you want me there now?' I ask looking at the paper. 'What about The Radstock Centre?'

'I did it online, they hadn't been hacked at all, someone had just inadvertently turned off the security protocols.'

'So it wouldn't run as a precaution.' Wil nods knowingly. 'See, you're getting it.'

Wil smirks, I was going to buy you lunch but I'm to discuss strategy with the Chief.' He nods back in the direction of the office that he's just left. 'Look if you can start now that will be excellent and you're in a suit yes, go for it.'

My career in the Civil Service doesn't start too brilliantly as nobody's told the guy on the door that I'm coming (although he cheerfully lets in members of the public with enquires.) Eventually an SCO (whatever that is) comes to get me, she's called Ray and Ray looks tired.

The office in question is called the Valuation office; it's essentially where the government assess the value of property. The value that they set determines the amount that the local authority will charge in rates for non domestic and which band the property sits in for domestic council tax (see I do pay attention.)

The real eye opener however is the Civil Service itself, I'm expecting old guys in three piece suits working from armchairs with waiters bringing food and drinks in an office that's all tranquillity and leisure.

For the uninitiated, successive governments generally portray the civil service in this way, usually before they take a hatchet to its annual budget.
The reality I discover is around two dozen mostly young and certainly stressed staff trying to do the work of over sixty.

There's always a mood, a *feel* to an office. Some are relaxed and calm and therefore successful and productive. This one just feels like the battle is long lost and it's running on empty.

Stress increases the levels of sickness, sickness increases the level of absence which adds to the levels of stress put onto those that remain.

Someone has hacked into their database. Their one IT guy is off on long term sick leave following a nervous breakdown the other walked a week ago.

Their head office is so short staffed that they've got nobody to send so they've had to get somebody locally which is me.

I sit at the computer praying that it isn't going to be a long job but I soon discover that it will be.

'Is all the data lost?' Mandy the staff officer peers over my shoulder, she's barely thirty but she looks exhausted and she's obviously been crying (although I suspect not about this.)

'What they've done is to delete it,' I tell her, 'but that isn't as bad as it sounds.' I add quickly. 'The computer can't throw the information away. So when you empty the recycle bin or the computer removes a file what it actually does is to remove the reference to the file on the hard drive. Once the header or reference is removed the computer can no longer see it so the space that the file took up is no longer reserved for it and any new file can be saved there which will overwrite it.'

'That's why your office told us not to save anything?'

'I nod,' I can use data recovery software to rebuild the file header as long as nothing was saved over it first.'

'So you *can* fix it?'

'I can get the information back and return it to the database, that's only a couple of hours. The other problem that you've been having, the changing speed and switching off monitors is a virus, that will take longer.'

'So somebody here . . ?'

'Clicked on a link, probably perfectly innocent but if you're not sure where the link is going, don't click it.'

'As quick as you can please.' She tells me patting me on the shoulder before she's dragged away to another problem.

I get my head down and get on with it. The staff are all really friendly but all clearly up against it. On top of the work load there's never ending ringing telephones and members of the public turning up at the counter. Here they keep their finger on the bell and are then, seemingly, entitled to verbally abuse and scream at whichever member of staff goes to the counter.

On the second morning this one guy is so obnoxious to a seventeen year old called Trish that she returns to the office in tears. I sit there fuming and trying to work out if there's any way that I could sneak out, beat him up in the lift and then sneak back without anyone noticing.

There isn't.

Lunchtime I sit in the staffroom with six of them asking them why they do it when one of the clerical officers called Julie storms in.

'Forty seven bloody minutes!' She snarls, hurling her mobile into a bag and pulling a pot noodle out of it.

As one we ask her what's taken forty seven minutes.

'I went out with one of the valuers this morning, assessing the new bedsits behind Corporation road.'

We all nod.

'So Jamie's chatting with the landlord and I'm stood like a lemon holding the tape by his car.

We all nod again.

'Well there's a group of guys chatting round the stairwell behind the pub and one of 'em says he's gonna do the priest at St Mikes, tonight.

'Why ever would anyone want to do that?' Trish says, clearly shocked.

'He's the guy who runs the food bank isn't he?' I ask looking up from my own pot noodle. 'I've worked down the citizen's centre they're always sending people around to him.'

Julie nods, she's still agitated, you can tell by how she's

stirring her food.

'From what I could gather, the priest got this guy's girlfriend into a safe house and wouldn't tell him where that was.'

'Did you tell the police?' I ask innocently.

'Oh yeah!' Julie throws her fork across the room into the sink. 'You can't ring 999 cos it's not an emergency so you ring 10 bloody 1.'

'Forty seven minutes?'

'She nods, 'and then when I do get through to somebody I get a woman who talks to me like I'm seven, oh he was probably showing off to his mates if he was going to do something he'd have done it when they argued.'

'So they're not going to do anything?'

'She said they'd log the call and if there was anyone in the area they'd look in on the church tonight if time permitted.'

'Should we ring him? Trish suggests. 'The priest.'

Julie shakes her head, abruptly realising she needed the fork for her food. 'He insists that the church is always open, he'd turn up even if he knew somebody was coming for him.

I pull a fork out of the draw and hand it to Julie. 'Let's hope he's got a guardian angel watching over him then.'

It feels like it's been ages since I've been out, the night air is cold and swirling around the roof of the church under a bright full moon which from my vantage point looks close enough to touch.

It's an old church, gothic you'd call it, it's got gargoyles. I stand beside them and practice looking broodily down at the streets below. You can never find a comic artist when you need one.

The priest is alone in his church below sorting through donated clothing, I didn't think to ask Julie what the guy looked like and I don't want to go jumping on anyone before they enter as they could be genuine and looking for help. Equally I don't want the wrong person to get too close maybe I should move closer.

Even as I'm debating this, the problem is solved, the bad guys turn up and are blindingly obviously up to no good.

They are also, clearly, inept.

Their bad guy car of choice is a smart little Hyundai, perfect for someone who's just passed their driving test but not good for five large lads armed with baseball bats. One scrambles up the steps whilst three more struggle to extricate themselves from the back seat. I'm down the side of the church and beside the car as the church door closes.

Now the driver is sat in place revving the engine and he sees me. Instantly he rams the car into gear and races (ish) away. The problem is two of his mates are only half way out of the back and both are flung violently out of the rapidly reversing car and onto the cobbled street. The front wheel of the car goes over the elbow of one of them with a sickening crunch and a scream. The guy who got out first looks at the guy screaming on the floor, looks at me and then faints. I kid you not, he drops like a sack of potatoes.

I glance quickly around the square in front of the church, there's three guys down, two unconscious, one screaming and the Hyundai slams backwards into a lamp post a hundred yards down the street

I haven't done anything yet!

I hurry up the steps and into the church, the *leader* of the gang is monologing and brandishing his bat, he has his back to me. The priest is on his knees surrounded by boxes of clothes, he's seen me but he doesn't react until I get right up behind the guy.

'You don't have to hurt him.' He tells me calm as you like. The guy spins round and swings the bat at me but it's all slow motion. I grab his right hand with my left and crush his fingers into the handle of the bat as I punch him unconscious with my right. He does his own sack of potatoes impersonation.

'You didn't have to do that!' The priest tells me with a sour expression and a hint of an Irish accent.

'I think I did.' I reply unimpressed.

'You've broken all of his fingers.' The priest tells me bending over the guy.

'I've broken four of the fingers of his right hand, they'll mend soon enough but it will be painful. Whilst they're mending he won't be slapping his girlfriend around nor picking on unprotected clergy and who knows maybe he'll take the opportunity to revalue some of his life choices.' The priest turns the guy onto his side and puts him into the recovery position. 'No clergy are unprotected.'

'Yeah well I didn't notice any armed angels on the way in.' I reply, I can't quite figure the priest.

'But I was protected.' The priest tells me firmly, he stands up straight and looks me in the eye. 'Or are you going to tell me that you were just passing.'

He's got me there, I smile under my mask and he smiles back even though he couldn't have seen it.

'I'd offer you tea or even a nip of something stronger but I have a feeling that you'll be wanting to leave. He nods over my shoulder and when I look I see a flashing blue light through the windows.

I nod to him and sneak out the back way except I don't, I scramble up and onto the roof over the back door and crouch down between the gargoyles.

The 'lads' are carried to a police van as all of the ambulances are tied up again, the priest gives a statement and a detailed description.
'It were a tall fella with a mask over his face.'
'Was it a skull,' a copper asks him wearily.
'Not altogether sure, could have been, it all happened so fast.'

Within twenty minutes the police are done and driving away, the priest returns to his church.
I sneak in silently watching him from the shadows at the back. There's no way that he can see me and I haven't made a sound but . . .
'Tea or Coffee?' He asks, without looking around.

The Priest – Chapter eleven

'Coffee two sugars,' I answer quietly, stepping out of the shadows.

'You made a right mess of that lads forearm outside,' he tells me as he stamps towards a door at the back of the church which leads to a tiny white tiled kitchen.

'I didn't actually do anything outside, I just dropped beside the car and the driver panicked, he threw it into reverse and shot off whist two of them were only half out. The third one fainted.'

The priest turns from filling his kettle and looks me up and down. 'Must be your after shave lad, there's a tin hidden behind those books.' He nods towards a shelf. 'You can have *one!*'

'I'm honoured,' I tell him palming a chocolate biscuit from the tin.

'That guy on tunnel terrace?' He says grabbing two mugs. 'He needed reconstructive surgery you know?'

'I know, it was the same sort of thing, I stopped the car lifted it up and dropped it, he fell out of the back onto his face.' I answer. 'They had just roughed up . . .'

'I know Janie at the centre and I know what they did.' He answers, it's hard to know what he's thinking, he's got an open face and an honest face but I can't read him. 'What's more I think I know what you're doing and why you're doing it, I'm just not sure I know how I'm supposed to react to it.'

'I don't think turning the other cheek works on the street Father.'

'It's Patrick, Pat to my mates. Turning the other cheek is a principle,' he reaches for the kettle that is boiling. 'In the context that it was used it was all about stopping the cycle of retaliation, you slap him, so he punches you, so you take a knife to him so then he brings a gun to you. If you just turn from the first slap it stops all the other things from coming.'

'But you get slapped a lot.' I point out and he smiles.

'Let's try it another way,' he hands me a mug and cradles his own as he leans back against the draining board. 'As a Christian I believe that all life is sacred, thou must not kill right?'

I nod and raise the bottom part of my mask to sip the coffee, he makes no attempt to look.

'But what am I to do if somebody else is about to kill and I'm able to stop them and in a position to stop them. What if I do nothing?'

'Then you're as guilty as the killer surely.'

He nods and takes another sip. 'So let's say I can talk the guy down, reason with him. I save the would be victim and I save the would be perpetrator. All nice and neat and home in time for tea.'

I take another sip, this guy's growing on me.

'But what if I can't talk him out of it? I can't talk him out of it but I'm bigger than he is and I'm stronger than he is, what then? I can't fight the enemy using the weapons of the enemy, I'm not supposed to use force but if I don't act an innocent will be hurt and probably killed.'

'Then it's the lesser of two evils,' I answer quietly.

'And that's where you're at I'm guessing.' He smiles slowly but his smile is completely genuine.

I nod slowly. 'There are so many that only understand *one* language.'

'And you're fluent.' He reaches for the chocolate biscuits and I start on mine.

'Do you believe in God son?'

'I chuckle and take another sip of the coffee. 'My head would say that is a ridiculous antiquated concept but . . .'

'But?'

'This goes no further?'

'I'm a Priest lad and it's not just for the confessional.'

'The circumstances that increased my strength robbed me of all of my memories, amnesia like you see in the films. I lost all of myself, I literally don't know who I am, I've had to rediscover all of it. So, I love movies, I love a curry, I prefer bitter to lager and coffee to tea except for those times when it has to be tea and I believe in God. It makes no sense to me whatsoever but in my heart I'm as sure as I can be.'

He nods slowly, smiling like a fool, then his face falls. 'You know how this will end don't you lad?'

I shake my head as I finish the biscuit.

'That Barclay guy was a monster, some of his girls were only fourteen, like a cancer in the neighbourhood, sucking the heart and soul out of it, bleeding it dry as he dines with the elite. He was also a fool that didn't see you coming. Others won't make that mistake. I'm guessing you don't have spider sense or bat radar or x-ray vision?'

I shake my head.

'Then it'll be a sniper, high powered rifle, explosive head on the bullet to be sure because I'm guessing you're not bullet proof either.'

'I'm fast.'

He looks at me and raises his eyebrows.

'It's only a matter of time lad, you're making powerful enemies.' He takes a long sip from his mug, 'and you'll need to be fast if you're going after that lass.'

'What lass?'

'Dresses up like an insect and beats up security guards.'

'In Cardiff?'

'Here mate, she was in West London last night, it was on the six o'clock news.'

All of a sudden I've gone right off my coffee.

I make my excuse and leave but I don't get far. I'm heading for somewhere central and high, somewhere with a good view of the surrounding area.

But two minutes from the church, slap bang in the middle of my own neck of the woods, I hear a guy groaning.

He's lying beside a skylight on the flat roof of a new shopping centre, he's in a uniform but he's not police. I hurry over to him, the logo on his overalls tell me that he's a maintenance guy from the shopping centre. He's been given a right hiding and his left shoulder is clearly dislocated and causing him a great deal of distress.

'Hold still mate,' I carefully take hold of his upper arm. 'I think I can . . .

She comes from nowhere, a blur of green, she slams into the side of me like a truck and sends me flying onto and then through the skylight.

The shopping centre is new and hasn't officially been opened yet. It's got those flashy raised glass walkways that makes it look like the customers are walking on thin air. The glass is said to be virtually unbreakable but let me assure you that if you fall twenty feet or so onto it isn't!

I slam down onto it and it explodes beneath me and I'm falling again.

I twist to the side grabbing for what I hope is a wall but it's a glass shop front. It shatters as I fall into it, I've got too much momentum and I can't keep my feet and I fall head first into a concrete wall to the side.

I'm not sure how long I've been out, it only feels like seconds but there's blue lights outside every window of the centre below me and voices and flashing lights on the roof above. I get to my feet groggily and look around, I'm in one of those designer boutiques, it looks like a bomb has hit it.
There are racks of clothing all over the floor, all of the front windows are broken and I appear to have smashed the till which I landed on after head butting the wall.
I feel like I really need to sit down for a few moments, my side is bleeding heavily so is the top of my leg, worse my head is agony.
I stagger to the front of the shop.
'THERE!' The shout is above my head and is instantly followed by gunfire, three or four guns shooting continuously.
I leap back, I've got a real problem now, not only do I feel like death warmed up but the internal walls of the centre are smooth painted concrete, there's no climbing up or down.
The main doors two floors below burst open as another police fire arms team appear in a huddle, all of their guns pointed forward.

'Third floor directly under us.' One of the officers shouts from the skylight. 'We'll cover you from here, he can't get out.'

The team on the ground floor hurry for the staircase whilst I head for the back of the trashed boutique. There's always a back door right?

Wrong! Stockroom no outside door. I turn my attention to the panelled wall. The building is clearly a concrete and glass shell which is then divided up inside to create shops. The walls of these are hardboard, so I punch a hole in it and clamber through into the shop next door which is DVD's and computer games, there's no back room here either.

I creep to the front of the shop and peer out.

I can see five figures over the broken sky light shining torches down; they're watching the shop front next door.

The centre is basically a large rectangle with shops around the outside edges and staircases and escalators in the middle.

I see the line of shops opposite has a fire escape in the middle, I can't see this side but figure there has to be a matching one over here.

I punch another hole through another wall and crawl through it into a jewellery shop. Instantly a shrill alarm goes off, there's a great deal of shouting and the whole front window of the shop disintegrates under a hail of bullets from both groups of police.

I'm fortunately at the back of the shop and neither group has the angle to shoot any further in than the front three feet or so.

I punch through the next wall and clamber through, I'm in a large cafe. That means there has to be toilets and . . . Bingo! There's a backdoor which I pull open. The noise is hidden by the continues firing of both firearms teams who are demolishing the front of the shop next door.

I carefully open the door, there is a fire escape this side, the cafe is next to it and the toilets are in it. It's essentially a long concrete tunnel running to the multi storey car park that's next to the centre. There's a locked steel gate into the car park but it's only a padlock which snaps with barely a tug. I'm in the car park now but my problems aren't over, there's a dozen, that's a dozen! Police cars and vans all over the ground floor of the car park below. I mean where have they come from? You need one and there's nothing in the area then when you *don't* need them it's like a convention. What's more they're not staying there, teams of officers are hurrying up the steps towards my floor, presumably to get into the centre via the fire escape.

Now normally I'd just hurry for the roof and from there jump onto the roof of an adjoining building in order to escape. The problem here is there is only one adjoining building of the right height and that has a trigger happy firearms team on it.

I race to the back wall of the car park. It's breeze block, five feet high and open to the elements. I scramble over it and then cling on with my finger tips as the police arrive on the other side of the wall.

It's now that I realise my mistake, I'm clinging onto the outside of the building and nobody can see me. But what did I do with that padlock? I've left the steel gate open against the wall. It's not something you'd notice but if they spot the broken padlock and then look to see that the gates open they're going to realise that I'm here somewhere.

I can fight them but I feel bloody terrible and like the priest said I might end up stopping a bullet.

I hang there for what seems an age as the officer's creep along the tunnel en masse. They're all too focussed on getting into the centre to spot anything fortunately. I shuffle along the side of the building to the corner and then carefully make my way down.

A few feet away officers James and Hooper are putting on bullet proof vests (!) Hooper's on his mobile, delight and excitement ring in his voice. 'Oh we've got him this time Sir you mark my words, Alpha team say there's blood all over the floor and there's no way out!'

He sounds like a child who's discovered a super rare

Pokémon card in his latest pack. I'm sat between a buddleia bush and the outside wall, ten yards behind him. I want to stay put and I want to sleep but I know I've got to move. Sticking to the shadows I slink across a delivery road at the back of the car park and up onto the railway embankment. I feel bloody awful, there is still noise coming from the centre, even when I'm half a mile away but I can still hear the shouting and the shooting and what the hell are they shooting at?

The hospital is a mile to my right but it's midnight and it's a Friday, Casualty is going to be like a warzone. I'm trying to think, trying to plan but it's like I can't get my head into gear.

I reach the top entrance of the hospital which is on a hill, I know that Mary lives in one of the flats in the block behind the nurses home. If I could only work out which one? But even as I'm thinking it I see it.

It's like one of those moments you see in films, the heroes on the floor, he's out of ammunition and a German Tiger tank is rattling towards him. Then from nowhere, there's angelic music and a P51 wallops the Tiger as the air force arrive in the nick of time.

Okay there's no angelic music (nor P51 for that matter) but there is a white Ford KA with a blue filler cap cover (her original was nicked but Angie scrounged a replacement from the local scrappy for her.) Even better than seeing her car is seeing where its parked, its parked in a numbered bay and the number is seventeen, she lives in flat seventeen!

I stagger towards the block, outside is a laminated plan of the complex showing where all the flat are, it's like it's my birthday! She's on the third floor, right hand side, far corner. I hurry around to look at the side of the building, there aren't balconies, but there is a raised line of paler bricks running under the windows making stripes along the side of the building.

I look to Mary's window the lights are on, she still up. I scramble to the corner of the building to the third floor and then carefully across the paler bricks. I can only get the end of my toes onto the narrow edge but it's enough, I gingerly shuffle across to her window.

It's a net curtain and this close up I can see through it, she's wearing just a long tee shirt and drying her hair with a towel, dancing and singing along to Abba (Abba?) my heart skips a beat, I've got to ask her out. I knock gently on the window.

She shrieks and jumps back staring at the window in shock. I give her a little wave.

'You maniac, what are you doing here?' She hisses opening the window with wide eyes.

'Please tell me you've got your kit,' I answer weakly, as the headache finds another gear.

She opens the window wide and steps back, 'I've always got my kit I'm a community nurse.' She whispers, 'what have you . . . oh there's blood all over you, get in the bath.'
'The bath?'
'I don't want blood on my carpet and don't make a sound.' She points me to the bathroom. 'If Matron hears you she'll have my hide, men aren't allowed.'
'Quite right too,' I tell her staggering into the bathroom and stepping into the bath.

Everything in the room is yellow, the china on the bath and the sink, the wallpaper and the blinds, there's even a lemon air freshener, its like being inside a giant lemon.
 'Guessing I know what your favourite colour is.'
'Shirt off, don't say it and I've only just got the flat. health authority initiative, they want us local but none of us can afford the rent in the area.' She watches me struggle to pull my leathers over my mask.
'God what have you done to yourself?' She hisses unzipping a large grey bag.
'Mantis threw . . .'
'Whisper.'
'Mantis threw me through a skylight. I went to help this guy on the roof . . .'
'Your leg's bleeding too, take your trousers off.'
I stare at her in sudden panic

She puts her hands on her hips and raises her eyebrows, 'you've not got anything on under them have you?'

'Um . . .'

'Have you?'

'It gets really hot wearing leather everything,' I answer lamely. 'It all tends to ride up and . . .'

'You do realise that I am a nurse don't you,' she pulls an antiseptic aerosol spray from her bag and sprays my side.

I scream like a twelve year old girl.

Mary isn't impressed, 'you utter . . . you complete . . .' words fail her for a moment.

Seconds later there's a bang on the door, 'Mary are you alright.'

Mary gives me a look that would silence a politician.

'Tell her I'm forcing you.'

There's another knock on the door.

I hear her open it, 'you better come in,' she says, 'you better see for yourself.'

Matron Myfanwy Hardcastle looks every inch the matron, she's five foot nothing in both directions and she is clearly not amused.

'YOU!' She snaps, 'what are you doing with my Sister?'

'What you're related?' I ask genuinely surprised then I get it.

'Look I needed a Nurse and I can hardly walk into Casualty can I?'

'So you're forcing this poor girl . . .'

'I'm not forcing her, I asked her to help, I've seen her in town, I know she's good and she doesn't turn people away. I recognised her car and worked out which flat was hers . . .'

'He's bleeding quite badly Myfanwy, ' Mary interrupts starting on my side.'

Myfanwy steps forward looking at my arm. 'You've had needlework on your arm recently.' She pulls a pair of glasses from her top pocket and puts them on to examine the scars.

'Cardiff,' I answer quickly, before Mary has to. 'I got into a fight with a psycho that had a Samurai sword.

'And that cut on your side?'

'Same psycho, pushed me through a skylight.'

Myfanwy nods. 'Do you know how many people you've sent to us?'

'Do you know what they were doing before I sent them to you?' I reply.

'I've got one man who's only just out of physiotherapy now, you attacked him on Black Bream lane six months ago.'

'Skinny fella, spiky red hair, seeing you on day release?'

She nods.

'And where is he now?' I ask unimpressed.

'How should I know . . . '

'He's back inside, I caught him after he'd dragged a schoolgirl from her Mother's car, she tried to run for it and he punched her in the mouth. I lost my temper a bit with that one I admit but somebody has to do something.'

'Oh that's why you do it?' She smirks, her tone ringing with sarcasm.

'I'm doing it because I can and because nobody else is.'

'What do you think the police are for.'

'The police are chronically under-staffed and under-funded, what officers they have are forced to spend the bulk of their time at their desks filling in forms. When was the last time you saw a copper out on the beat?'

'We are a civilised society, there are ways and means . . .'

'We are a civilised society that is no longer working the way that it should. You represent the NHS which is amongst the very best that we're capable of and look at the truth of it.' I snap grimacing against the headache which is like an orchestra in my head. 'People spending hour after hour on a trolley or in an ambulance and that's if they can get an ambulance. Over the pandemic everything else went out of the window, people in the middle of life saving urgent treatment where every day is crucial suddenly had to wait for months and now waiting lists are longer than they ever have been.' I snap back getting hot under the collar.

'I should go and call the police.' She answers but she's calmer.

'Go and call them then,' I reply unimpressed. 'If any turn up in time I'll beat them up if I have to.'

'I can call Mary away from you now, where would you be then?'

'You could call her but she wouldn't come, she wouldn't come because she's a *proper* nurse, she has a duty of care and that means something to her. She may not approve of my methods but she knows that I'm just trying to keep people safe. Hand on my heart, I'll never start a fight but I won't stand by when people are being walked over.' I glare at the woman, my head's killing me and she *so* isn't helping.

Myfanwy however surprises me, rather than turning on her heel and grabbing the nearest phone she turns her attention to my leg.

'There's a lot of blood here too Mary.'

'I've told the gentleman to remove his trousers but he's shy.' Mary answers, this time giving me daggers with her voice but I can see laughter in her eyes.

'Oh for goodness sake!' Myfanwy thrusts her hands to her belt. 'If you can stand against the forces of evil you can remove your trousers in front of two experienced nurses who've seen far more than you can imagine or are likely to have.' She grabs the antiseptic aerosol with a menacing expression.

Reluctantly I remove my boots then my leggings and quickly try to maintain my dignity with a well positioned flannel.

'You're boot is full of blood,' Myfanwy upends it in the sink and hastily washes her hands. 'And look at the state of that leg!'

'Will you keep still!' Mary snaps, as I squirm under her needle. 'No wait a minute, you're swaying, shaking, did you bang your head?' She adds, suddenly all concern again.

'I was out for a minute or two after I head butted a concrete wall.' I admit.

'Out? You mean unconscious?' Both nurses ask in unison.

'Yeah but only a minute or two, I think.'

'You need to take the mask off.' Mary tells me sternly, her hands on her hips now.

'No.' I answer firmly, the harder I try not to sway the more I actually do.

'Young man, if you were unconscious only for a second there is a real danger of concussion we have to check.

'No.' I tell them flatly.

'Look we won't tell anyone what you look like,' Myfanwy says.

'Don't you guys read?' I answer, 'don't you know what happens?'

Both of them look at me non-plussed for a moment. 'Well now I do quite like a little bit of Christina Rossetti and I caught Mary reading Jane Eyre the other day but the Perils of Wonderman I seem to have missed.'

'The Perils of Wonderman?!'

'Young man, we're grown mature intelligent women,' Myfanwy barks, 'we don't read comics.'

'This is real life not a comic' Mary says reaching for my mask.

'You don't know and you don't see the people that I deal with, oh you see the underlings, those at the bottom of the food chain, you don't see what's at the top. There is real evil in this world anonymity is the only protection that I have for myself and anyone that I know. I am *not* removing my mask.' I lean back away from Mary's hands clinging onto my flannel for dear life.

'Let me put my hands under the back of your mask then,' she says quietly. 'I won't remove it you have my word.' I lean forward and she slides her hand up the back of my mask and gently over the back of my head as Myfanwy applies herself to my thigh.

So I'm standing there, I've got the girl of my dreams stood in front of me (in her bath) with her arms around me feeling the back of my head. There's only a flannel between us. She smells of chanel and hair shampoo and there isn't a guy on the planet who could describe her without using the word gorgeous and it's just feels wrong. I'm not free, I belong to somebody else but how can I?'

'You've got a hell of a bump there,' Mary says unimpressed.

'Get home, sleep, then go and see your GP in the morning, tell him you fell downstairs and knocked yourself out. He'll examine you properly.'

'I will, first thing.' I lie.

'Will you tell me something?' Myfanwy looks up from her needle work.

'If I can.'

'If you're a superhero why do you wear such a god awful mask?'

'Yeah fair question,' Mary agrees returning to her own needlework. 'Your look is more super villain.'

I sigh, 'it is to engender fear in the forces of evil,' I repeat, I've already had this conversation with Mary and it gets lamer each time. 'It's a lovely name, Myfanwy I mean, its Welsh isn't it? I ask taking a stab at changing the subject.

'Aye not that far from Cardiff.'

'Yeah, I liked Cardiff.'

'Beat up many on your visit did you?' Myfanwy asks unimpressed.

'I saved an undercover WPC who got thrown off a roof then got a kicking from the psycho with a sword.'

'See,' Myfanwy says wistfully looking up to Mary, 'when I visit somewhere I'd rather look at the sights then go for a meal.'

'Oh I had a super pizza there, guy made it on a brazier.'

'Not Harry, up by the castle with a black barrow.' Myfanwy

asks with interest, looking up from her stitching.

'One arm and a patch over his eye?'

'That's him, I nursed him in Port Talbot in the nineties.'

'When you were a student?'

Myfanwy laughs and her expression lightens.

'Superb Pizza.' I add.

'He was half Italian on his mother's side . . . what do you want?'

When Myfanwy came in she left the door to the flat and the bathroom door open wide. There's now three student nurses looking in and they're apparently surprised to see a blood covered man naked save for a flannel and a bright green rather tasteful skull mask being stitched up in the bath by two nurses one of whom is on her knees.

'Nothing to see here girls, you should be in bed its gone midnight and you've got exams tomorrow.' Myfanwy says calmly returning her attention to my leg.

'Matron do you realise who that is?' The one in the middle gasps as the two on either side of her brandish their mobiles.

'Oh I'm not him, it's just a costume for my stag night but some guy pushed me through a window.' I tell them.

They hurry away, I'm not entirely sure that they're convinced.

'So this Mantis what has she got against you?' Mary asks calmly, like we're chatting down the pub.

'She's looking for something and she doesn't care who she has to hurt to get it.'

'Does she wear a costume too?' Myfanwy asks from somewhere around my knee. Her stitches are so small and neat that my leg looks like its got a zip but she's nowhere near as quick as Mary.

'Haven't you seen her?' I reply surprised, 'she's been on the news.'

'I always turn it off when they do the silly stuff.'

'What's she like?' Mary asks, pausing to spray more antiseptic onto my side which she's just finished then handing the tin to Myfanwy.

'She's French, volatile, lovely figure.'

'Lovely figure?' Mary queries sharply doing the dagger thing with her eyes again.

'Apparently.' I answer lamely.

'What's she looking . . . oh for goodness sake.' Myfanwy blurts as a police siren sounds outside and a car skids to a halt. The voices of the three student nurses can be heard all talking at once.

'Oh for goodness sake!' I fall back against the cold tiled wall behind me and almost lose my flannel.

'Don't worry,' Myfanwy hauls herself to her feet handing the needle to Mary. 'I'll send them way, I'll stick to the idiot on his stag night story that's completely believable.' She bustles from the room but I'm not having it, I grab my trousers.

'How the hell did they get here so quickly?'

'Friday and Saturday night they always have a couple of cars here outside Casualty and you can't go yet, your leg is only half done.'

'Mary they're not going to buy it, they'll be up here in a minute, there isn't time.'

'Okay, I'll finish it with staples.'

'You'll do what?'

'I'll staple it.'

I look at her horrified, she isn't joking and now she's delving into her bag.

Fortunately, it turns out that not all staplers are for paper. It turns out that there are medical staplers as well for sealing wounds.

'The spray cleans and helps with the pain for stitches but this will hurt I'm afraid.' Mary tells me holding up the device that looks like something out of a Hammer film.

'Don't worry,' I tell her heroically, 'just be quick.'

'The stitches will dissolve like before but you'll need to see me to remove these, don't come here though.' She gives me those eyes again then applies herself to her dreadful task.

However as she finishes and I'm trying to juggle my trousers and the flannel, Myfanwy reappears as calm as you like.

'They believed you!' I gasp astounded.

'They told us that the Vigilante had been arrested earlier on this evening, so you were indeed an idiot on his stag night.'

'They what?!' I gasp.

'Arrested,' Myfanwy tells me, handing me my boots.

'Was there anyone else with you?' Mary asks, putting her tools into the sink.

'No, it was that new shopping centre, it's not open yet.' I hand the flannel back to her. 'Thanks for that.'

'It's my *face* flannel,' she tells me snatching it off me.

'Look I've got to scoot.' I pull my top over my mask.

'You need to rest and don't fight Mantis until those staples are out.' Mary says.

'You are not leaving by the front door!' Myfanwy says.

'Oh Myfanwy,' I tell her sweetly, 'I never leave by the front door.'

I'm home in quarter of an hour, and really careful for the last stretch. I feel bloody terrible, I crawl up the side of creepy crags like a little old man and fall from the windowsill.

Even Pablo seems concerned as I crawl into the kitchen and stash my suit.

A couple of prawns help him feel better and a flashing light on the landline tells me that I've got twenty seven missed calls, Adam no doubt.

I think I here a knock on the door as I fall into bed but I

really don't care, I *have* to sleep.

Five minutes later the light is on and somebody is shaking me.

'What the hell has happened, the News said you've been arrested, I thought I told you to lie low and . . .'

I grab his wrist with a snarl and squeeze, part of me wants to tell him about what I've discovered about my dad but that still small voice inside tells me no.

'Steve, my wrist!' Adam yelps, so I let him go.

'Adam I need to sleep I'm done in.'

'What happened?' He snaps back rubbing his wrist. 'Look at the state of you.'

'Mantis.'

'What about the stuff I gave you?'

'I didn't get the chance to use it, she hit me from nowhere.'

'You should be more careful, you should . . .'

'No Adam,' I grab his wrist again. 'Turns out it's not like the comics mate, I don't have spider sense and I can't always see them coming.'

'You're supposed to be lying low, I mean this and that Barclay guy . . .'

'I said on the blog Adam I dropped into his room to have a chat with him and there's all of these people some with guns.'

He pulls himself away, angry himself now. 'No this has gone far enough now, I'm taking back your costume for a couple of months then we'll see about . . .'

'Adam if you can find my costume your welcome to it, you can take it, just leave your spare key to the flat on the dish by the door.'

I drop back on my pillow turning my back on him, in moments I'm gone.

I'd intended to ring in sick but hadn't thought to switch off the alarm. So at 7.30AM I'm up and staring blearily around the room.

One of the plusses with *my condition* is that I recover really quickly. I felt like I was going to die last night but now I just feel kind of rough around the edges.

I get up shower and dress, noting that Adam's key is indeed in the dish. The news tells me that more vagrants have disappeared, a local charity is convinced that something sinister is going on. The local MP says that they've probably just moved out of the area. A couple of tablets and a good breakfast and I'm ready for the Civil service again.

I don't bother checking to see if Adam found the suit because I know that he hasn't. I've got the perfect hiding place, I've also got a second costume, completely different that Adam knows nothing about.

Before I got the job with Wil I got freelance work for a week or so with a production studio down by the river. I told them I'd done stunt work but had lost my papers in a house fire. They asked me to show them what I could do and soon as I did they were paying me £700 a day. Easiest money I've ever made in my life, they dressed me in clothes from a charity shop gave me a mask and got me to jump out of windows onto an air bag.

It sounds glamorous but in truth you're just sat in a chair waiting for hours on end. Finally then, you get to do your thing, the director says it was perfect then makes you go again and again.

At the end of it all the only person I'd really got to know was the costume maker, she was a single Mum and only being paid a pittance so I gave her £200 for the mask and the clothes she was elated. Not sure I'll ever need them but if I do, I'll tell you all about it.

Then breaking news says that the Vigilante has been captured by police and is in custody. A grinning Home Secretary tells the cameras outside Downing street that she'll be making a statement later.

I spend a thrilling morning in the Valuation office, there is chaos all around me but my software's been working overnight as the database is whole and sound once more. Next task is to locate the virus which is likely hidden in a directory somewhere, this potentially could take ages but I find it in an hour. It looks like supreme skill but its sheer dumb luck!

I'm out of there by lunch time and sat in a pub with a lamb bhuna and a pint watching the one o'clock news.

There's a brief summary to begin with, the Home Secretary to start, then more missing person reports, then Wally the Walrus has been spotted in the Thames.

It cuts to the Home Secretary who's stood at a podium with a grin that stretches from ear to ear. There's a dozen uniformed officers stood to attention behind her. The phrase cat that's got the cream springs to mind.

'Ladies and gentlemen,' she begins milking the moment. 'We've got him!'

There's some polite applause.

'Acting on a tip off last night,' she continues, eyes fixed on her autocue, two specialist firearms teams backed up by nearly fifty uniformed officers cornered the fugitive in the new Spendwell shopping centre. After an intense gun battle and stand off with the police he was apprehended at around

11pm last night.' She stands back with the smuggest of smiles.

'Home Secretary,' It's Penny, she's in with the first question like a ferret up a drain pipe. 'We've spoken to store owners who were in the centre this morning and they said that the whole of one side of the third floor looked like a warzone. Hundreds of thousands of pounds worth of stock destroyed in the fire fight but the vigilante doesn't use a gun.'

Any-Man Penny, it's Any-Man.

'I can't discuss operational methods or procedures with you Penny but I do agree that a great deal of damage was done to a brand new centre that hasn't even opened yet and this I'm afraid is what happens when amateurs attempt to take the law into their own hands.'

The reporter next to Penny flies in. 'Can you confirm that the Vigilante was shot?'

I choke on my beer.

'He was,' she answers, still smiling. 'Whilst attempting to flee the scene he was challenged by officers and then shot in the shoulder. Despite all the things that he has done, all the laws that he has broken, all the people that he has put in hospital. My officers went out of their way to ensure that he was taken alive and with the minimum amount of harm.'

'Can't you tell us who he is?' Penny again, she's like a dog with a bone.

'Penny we obey and we respect the laws of the land, this man clearly doesn't despite this we will still ensure that he is dealt with fairly and by the book. He has shown contempt for the system, we will be obedient to it and we will respect the law despite all of his provocation. Accordingly I cannot reveal his name or details at the moment not until he's officially charged and that can only be after he's recovered from surgery. However I can tell you that he is male, he is thirty two years old and in his past he was a member of her majesties armed forces. I can also tell you that he has a police record and has had frequent dealings with the police throughout his life.'

This excites the room, and gets most of the journalists on their feet, all shouting questions at once.

The Home Secretary picks one with a pointed finger, like a child in a sweet shop.

'Home Secretary where will he be detained, how can he be held?' A young reporter who looks about twelve blurts out quickly.

'He is currently under armed guard at a military hospital which I'm obviously not going to name. As soon as he's ready he'll be moved to secure accommodation.'

'Home Secretary,' Penny again, seriously somebody should

give this girl a costume. 'Given what's been happening in several different places that have been given the title of secure accommodation, do you think that's wise?'
Penny's done it again, the smile falls and anger flashes in the Ministers eyes. 'No more questions.' She stomps away from the microphones as the uniforms peel after her like a military display flight.
I saunter out of the pub and enjoy the sunlight and fresh air. The office tells me that Wil needs me to pop back to the Special needs Primary and install some software for them.

That's done by early evening and I'm walking through crowded streets lost in thought. I can't go in and rescue the guy even though I'm sure I could find him.
The police have still got search teams crawling over the shopping centre, I'm guessing they're looking for the costume. They must have stumbled on the guy at the scene and assumed he'd ditched the costume and was trying to get away.
My best bet is to get home, suit up then make sure I'm seen and even as I'm thinking this something rather wonderful happens.
Earlier on I found a virus in no time and the same thing has just happened again.
There's a kid, five maybe, he's shouting and raging, his Mum and Dad are dragging him along the street, clearly

furious.

'It was, it was,' he shouts with the conviction that can only come from complete honesty. 'It was her, I saw her she's there.' He points again to the top floor windows of a solicitors office across the road. 'It was her.'

'Don't be so silly David,' the Mother snaps. 'This is what comes of reading comics late at night!'

'But Mum it was her, it was Mantis!'

Chapter twelve - Showdown

I'm home in seven minutes, running as fast as I dare. So much for resting the leg.

Two minutes to get the costume in a bag and walk out whistling after waving to Alf.

Another seven to get back, into an arcade behind the offices, into the public toilet, costume on, clothes and shoes into bag. Out of the window and onto the roof where I stash the bag, its early evening and not dark yet.

Of course it could just be a secretary trying on a costume for the boss, probably best not to go charging in.

The offices below are all in darkness, its gone six so the staff are gone, there's a cafe outside below, tables on the pavement, tourists everywhere.

Thing is, why would she be inside? She'd be on the roof surely and these buildings are old but they are brick not stone. I start to wonder if the Oxford professor was spinning me a yarn.

I'm in through a skylight, there's a central hall, lots of marble and black and white tiles. I've got the tablet under my belt, I switch it on then run the program that I've prepared before tucking it back under my belt. I creep along listening at doors, then abruptly a door across the hall opens, a young woman steps through staring at her mobile phone. A young woman dressed in green and with two swords in scabbards crossed on her back.

Twice she's got the jump on me, not this time.

'MANTIS!' I run straight at her, startled she drops her phone and snatches a sword from her back but even then she's fast enough to swing it at me.
I block it with my left wrist, I've got both of the guards and the magnets on. The blade strikes with a clang then sticks catching her completely off guard. I jerk the blade down with my left hand whilst I'm drawing the metal bar from behind my belt with my right. I slam the bar down onto the top of the blade with every ounce of strength that I have. The blade doesn't break it shatters. Mantis screams, it hurts my ears for a second cos she's so loud.
'Cretin!' She screams.

Meaning cretin, imbecile or moron.

The tablet announces from my belt.

'Imbécile!'

Meaning Imbecile, fool, idiot, colloquially, moron or jerk

She grabs the other sword and swings it at my head, I block it with the iron bar, making her scream again
'Pourquoi interfères-tu?'

Literally why are you interfering? Or colloquially why are you sticking your nose into my business.

The tablet translates as I block two more strikes with the bar. 'I'm interfering because you are causing complete mayhem looking for a medieval book that probably doesn't exist.' I tell her then realise as she comes at me again that the translation software would have more effectively enabled a two way conversation if I'd included English to French as well as French to English
'Cretin!' She screams with real feeling and a vicious sideways thrust at my throat.

Cretin meaning cretin, imbecile or moron.

I block the sword again but this time I've pressed the button on the bar, the sword clangs and sticks throwing her off balance. I twist the bar mercilessly forcing it down, she releases it with another scream and the sword slams into the wall so hard that the hilt comes away from the blade. 'Espèce d'idiot, ces épées avaient deux cents ans!' She screams.

Meaning you bloody idiot those swords were two hundred years old.

It's just fists now, which should suit me but as I ram the bar back into my belt she punches me a dozen times across the head.

'Cretin, cretin, CRETIN!'

Literally moron, moron, moron.

She is so fast and she is strong, far stronger than anyone who's hit me before but I know instantly that she isn't strong enough. She can beat me on speed but I can take her for strength.

I lash out and punch her properly catching her left shoulder.

I have read up on this, I don't just do it. There are parts of the body that you can really wallop others where you have to be careful, you'll do real or permanent damage if you punch there too hard.

There's a nerve cluster on the shoulder, I won't be specific about its exact location but if you catch it right the whole arm goes dead.

I punch her here catching her perfectly, instantly her arm drops, it's not hanging right and her expression changes. The fury and rage is suddenly alarm.

She swings a kick at me but I block it with my elbow then drag it down her shin.

Then she slams her right hand into my face pushing my head back and twisting out of my arms as I try to grab her. My left hand closes on her belt and I swing her backwards into what I think is the wall but I've lost my bearings and it's a window. With a crash the two of us fall through it and down towards the street below.

I land on (an instantly demolish) an awning over the cafe, then I drop onto the pavement and inadvertently push a waitress with a full tray of drinks into the table she was approaching.

Mantis meanwhile misses the awning completely and slams full length into a row of tables that have been pushed together for a birthday party.

There are people everywhere!

The guy who's birthday it is, is stood there making a speech and preparing to blow out his candles. There's twenty at the table with him and twenty plus excited Japanese tourists surrounding them and photographing what to them is another fascinating local custom.

Part of the problem here is the way that she lands, through sheer dumb luck she pretty much lands along the length with her head on or rather in the cake, on the plus side the guy no longer needs to blow his candles out.

Things aren't a lot better on the table under the awning, there's half a dozen (very large) Rugby guys celebrating their latest triumph. When I send their waitress flying into their table and worse she tips the tray straining under the weight of all their drinks all over the lot of them.

This does not go down well.

As Mantis disappears under a swarm of photographers I disappear under about a tonne and a half of rugby muscle. Again, under normal circumstances this would be terrifying, these are *big* guys and they are not happy, but as I said before, it's toddlers with a tantrum, red faces, podgy fists, loads of noise and practically zero pain.
I drop onto my right hand and kick out my leg in a circle, kicking their legs from under them and dropping them like awkward tubby dominos onto the pavement.

Mantis meanwhile is, rather unsurprisingly, not enjoying the attention and leaps from the broken tables with a scream, showering the tourists with icing. The tourists however are still convinced that this is all part of the ritual; I guess they're assuming that it's all a variation on the girl popping out of the cake. They surround her taking photos and trying to get selfies.

As I send the rugby guys flying Mantis barges from the circle of photographers and dashes out into the road.

Unfortunately there is one of those tourist double-deckers which (thank God) is empty save for the driver, who's coming to pick up the tourists. She stamps on the brakes and steers into the kerb in a desperate attempt to avoid Mantis. Now the problem with these buses is stability and it turns out that slamming one violently sideways into the curb will tip it. On the plus side the height of the bus coupled with the narrowness of the pavement, leaves the top of the bus leaning, and ominously creaking, against the building rather than the whole thing lying on the pavement.

This still however causes complete pandemonium, cars behind the bus crash into each other, everyone on the pavement and everyone in the cafe run screaming in every possible direction as I free the driver from her cab.

Mantis meanwhile legs it along the road causing at least three more car collisions in the process.

Soon as I've got the driver out I'm after her, the arm is slowing her down a bit and the landing on the table clearly hasn't done her any favours but she's still a couple of hundred yards ahead of me.

Suddenly she's rugby tackled by a copper as she jumps from the road to an embankment that runs along the side of the river. Even as I race towards her as she beats the living daylights out of the copper, I'm also rugby tackled by a group of boys on a night out that clearly want to make a name for themselves. I bang the heads of the two most persistent ones together and throw a third one down a flight of subway steps.

I dash out into the road, hurdling a taxi and a fiat, it's still light (just) and there's people everywhere, so much for skulking about in shadows.

By the time I reach the copper he's unconscious and there's no sign of Mantis. In addition to this I have a second problem.

We're not that far from the centre of London and because of the bus and car collisions and our chase along the road there is now total gridlock. Amongst all of the stranded traffic is an Army lorry, a policeman, no doubt partner to the one that Mantis has just knocked out, is shouting into the back of the lorry and pointing in my direction. In all fairness I am leaning over what is for all he knows, the corpse of his colleague.

In seconds a dozen properly scary lads in camo gear are haring towards me like dogs after a rat. They're properly scary because each of them is brandishing an assault rifle.

I've got *one* option, it's to my left on the other side of the railing, I take a running leap and dive into the Thames. It's about as I hit the water that I remember that I don't know whether or not I can swim.

It turns out I can, I also know from experience that I can hold my breath for a good while as well. I turn up river staying underwater and swimming against the current, there were buoys that I saw when I dived so I try to head for these but even with my lenses I can't see a thing.

I surface after two minutes or so, just a quick gulp of air then keep just the top of my head from the eyes up above the surface.

I've come up much further than I thought, I can see a line of people along the railings, the squaddies and the copper. Every now and then the copper will point and shout and one or more of the squaddies will fire a burst but they're all looking straight out in front of them across the river, I'm quarter of a mile upstream, beside an old and very rusty buoy that bobs up and down beside me.

It's then as I look around properly that I realise I know where Mantis must be, because she will have done what I would have done.

Two large roads converge at a roundabout beside the river. Mantis was on what was originally the lower towpath. There's a large square of buildings in what is effectively now the middle of the roundabout but there's road or river on every side, the buildings are in effect an island.

The only way that Mantis could have disappeared would have been into the river on her left, in which case I would have seen her go. Or into those buildings and up onto the roof, that's what I would have done. The problem is once you're up there what do you do? Its not properly dark and the place is crawling with people. She can't flee across the rooftops because there's nowhere to flee to, it's just road and river below.

She's still there and she'll wait until its properly dark and properly quiet.

Which means that I've got to wait in, what a tourist brochure might say, the golden waters of the Thames. I think liquid mud is the word that best describes my bit.

It's surprising how long it takes for the crowd to clear and for the traffic to start moving again. If anyone leaves the buildings they can only go in one of two directions, I swim back to the side of the river and position myself where I can see both.

Finally I see her, she's taken her mask off and the helmet, she's carrying them like a handbag. Her arm isn't right and she's limping.

I pull myself from the river and keep low behind a small maintenance shed. I take my jacket off, shake it quickly then reverse it, then I pull off the mask, rolling it up and carrying it in my hand. I stay away from the street lights and follow her at a distance.

I soon realise that she's heading back towards the offices where we fought. She ducks down a lane, as I scramble up onto a wall pulling on my mask and from there a garage roof. This gives me a good view of the lane but she's disappeared again.

I'm up the corner of a house and onto the roof, a better view but I still can't see her.

We're not far from the offices now so I head back to check, I can't have let her get away again surely?

I hurry along the rooftop when I'm suddenly aware of an argument on the corner beneath me.

Outside a takeaway on the corner a gentleman who looks like an elderly and somewhat podgy Fu Man Chu is shouting loudly at somebody that I can't see.

'You no park there, that private parking, you been gone hours.'

A motorbike starts and revs loudly, craning my neck I get a glimpse of the bike which is bright green.

I'm down the side of the house like a squirrel on a promise, as I hear the bike start to move.

The old guy steps out into the middle of the lane stretching out his arms. 'You not leave til I have some cash!'

As the bike hurtles forward I'm on the ground and I hurl the bar at the front wheel. It jams the spoked wheel with a crunch and sends the back of the bike up into the air and the driver flying over the handlebars. Mantis slams into a bright red post box with the most appalling crunch.

The guy throws his hands up into the air, 'Oh Any Guy you've killed her.

I drop onto a knee beside her and grab her wrist as he leans over us. 'No she's out for the count but her pulse is as strong as an ox.' I tell him. 'And it's Any-Man.

'Good, she owes me money,' he says clearly relieved. 'Has she got a purse or a handbag with her?'

'See for yourself,' I tell him leaning back, 'her costume looks like it's been sprayed on, there's nowhere to hide anything.'

'Yeah?' He replies unimpressed, 'where did she get the keys for her bike from then?'

'You got me there.'

'Have you got handcuffs?' He asks.

'Not on me,' I admit. 'Have you got any cable ties in the shop?'

He nods, 'You tying her up with cable?'

I shake my head, 'just get me three.'

He disappears into the shop whist I take a quick photo of her to send to Adam.

'What good these?' He waves the plastic ties at me.

'They're strong as hell,' I tell him, 'and she's got a knackered arm. Right put one around her left wrist and close it.'

He does.

'Now put another around her right wrist and close it.'

He does.

I lift her carefully into a sitting position against a lamppost,
Then hold out her two arms behind her back and either side
of the lamppost. 'Right put the third one through both of the
others and push it closed.'

'Oh that's really clever.' Fu Man Chu tells me approvingly as
he does it.

We've gathered a small crowd now all filming us quietly
with the cameras.

'But how will I get my money?'

'Right what you need to do now, is to ring the police.'

'Yes.'

'Tell them that you've caught her and she's unconscious.'

'Yes.'

'Then when they get here tell them that you'd like a reward
and she owes you parking money on top of that. The police
have always got cash on them, they'll probably want to pay
you straight away and the bosses will probably want to
thank you in person.' I tell him as I retrieve my bar from the
broken bike wheel.

'How much monies will there be?' He asks turning from me
to the crowd.

'The papers will give you a fortune for your story.' One of
the girl shouts out from behind her camera phone.

I leave Fu Man Chu with his new fan club and within
seconds he's charging a tenner for 'a selfie next to bug lady.'

From a nearby rooftop I watch a police car and ambulance arrive together and cart off Mantis whilst the shop proprietor argues with the police about his money.

'C'est La Vie.' I say quietly as they drive her away.

Literally - Such is life.

I switch the Ap off and send Adam a text.

Guess what?

I send him the photo of Mantis unconscious.

Then text - *Those little extras made all the difference – thanks – NOW I'm going to take it easy!*

I felt mean about snapping at him, he hasn't been completely honest with me but I don't the reason and I do know that he's trying to help. Most of this is because of him, I don't have many friends and its silly to lose the one's that I have.

Within seconds he's ringing so I put in the earphones.

'You beauty, you absolute star, well done mate!' I can tell by his voice that he's as relieved as he is happy and I know I've made the right decision.

'It was your kit sunshine, the victory is yours as well. Those magnets worked a treat; the bar broke both swords and stopped her motorbike.'

Adam lets out a whoop of delight, all of a sudden he sounds about seven. 'And mate she's gorgeous and blimey her costume doesn't leave much to the imagination. How the hell did you concentrate on the fight?'

'It's surprising how the swords focus your mind mate.'

'You're all over the News son, they reckon you and she have broken London, you certainly broken the internet. Should have seen the reporters with the Home Secretary.'

'I'll watch the news when I get back, I'm still out, anything on the guy they arrested?'

'Yeah he was just some poor vagrant, he was bedding down in the car park and did a runner when he heard the police arrive.'

'Poor bugger.'

'The best of it was, when you were in Cardiff battling bug girl he was inside, so it obviously wasn't him, they only let the guy out last Thursday. Listen mate, please . . .'

'Adam you were right, I was cranky cos I felt bloody awful but I'm sorted now and thanks to you, things should be a lot quieter now.'

'Take a break Stephen.'

'I'm way ahead of you mate, Wil's given me a couple of days off I'm planning on sleeping through them.'
'Or taking somebody out, how's it going with Helen and Mary?'
'Bye Adam.'

The following morning sees me in the posh part of town. Wil's Mum is a style icon (the Palace consult her on chic according to Wil.) She's told me (via Wil) the best place to buy posh towels and flannels.
I spend an arm and a leg on an ultra posh matched towel and flannel (in discrete sunrise yellow)set then I order two very large (but properly tasteful) bouquets of flowers from Cheryl at the mini-mart.
I'm home for lunch and there's a parcel in front of the door. I hand Pablo some prawns then open it carefully.

When I found out about some of my past I soon found myself looking at fishing books online, specifically books on Tench fishing. Each time I saw the pictures on the cover it brought to mind what I had remembered. Then one evening I saw a book that made my heart jump because I knew I'd seen it before.
It was originally published back in the 1970's and there was a wonderful painting of a tench on the cover. I knew at once

that there was no colour inside, just text and line diagrams and a handful of black and white photos and I knew that the back cover was bright blue.

I had owned this book, at some point in the life that I have lost, I had bought, read and treasured this book.

I had to have it.

I paid £30 online and I'm sure I was ripped off but it didn't matter a jot. Now it's here and I open the package with trembling hands.

My first reaction to the book is disappointment, everything is exactly as I remember it except the size. The size is all wrong. I look inside the covers at the publishing history, all is how I remember it and there's only been one version so how can it be so small?

Then it hits me, the book hasn't got smaller, my hands have got larger, I was a kid the last time I picked it up.
The realisation stabs at my heart and I cradle the book in shaking hands. It's just a little pocket money book on fishing for tench but for me it is so much more, it's like I can take that kid, the kid I lost, the one that disappeared and I can hold his hand.
Now I know this sounds dumb but I just sit there like a

complete idiot nursing the book like Gollum with the ring and I flick through pages I've flicked through a thousand times before for the very first time.

Then there's a photo, a tench in the net being lifted from the water and suddenly I'm beside a different lake, this one surrounded by trees, I'm older than before but my hearts pounding just as quickly. This time the rods in my hands and I'm clinging onto it for dear life. My dad's at the water's edge and now he's got the net because this tench is mine. He turns from the water with the biggest smile on his face, he's so proud, 'Your first Tench mate,' he tells me laying the fish on the grass in front of me. 'Well played lad!'
I sit there staring at the book, for a whole hour I literally cannot put it down.

The following morning I'm up early and out, I do have a slight issue. Those staples Mary put in, well it turns out that a hard kick from psycho doesn't do them any favours, mind you she did tell me to take it easy.

Mantis is One Justine Jacques It occurred to me (eventually) that I'd been so elated that I'd taken her out of circulation that it didn't occur to me that I might have done her serious harm.

Her pulse was strong certainly but she was out cold, having taken a hell of a wallop from the post box.

The problem is I can stop most with (what is to me) minimum force. That wasn't the case with Mantis but it was only afterwards that I really considered just how hard I'd hit her.

The other side of this is around twenty security guards (probably all on minimum wage) hospitalised for simply doing their job. I know for a fact that at least two of them had what the BBC described as life-changing injuries and that can't be good.

France has apparently demanded Justine's extradition and I think the UK Home Office are more than happy to see the back of her.

Does leave me with quite a few questions though and in addition to these why was she searching *inside* those offices? The bit about capitals was obviously right but was the rest of it just a yarn to get me off Sandra's back?

I decide to spend the afternoon taking a hackers look at *Alsop, Rudd and associates*, the solicitors that Mantis raided.

For now though I'm in the minimart picking up the flowers from an exuberant Cheryl. I've got the top part of my costume in a carrier bag and soon I'm walking across to the clinic where Mary stitched me up after the bank job.

Fortunately the roof skylight is open, so I sneak into the lane behind the buildings and in less than a minute I'm onto the roof and in.

It's about twenty minutes till Mary gets in. There's an examination couch in the corner of the consulting room with a curtain screen. I pull back the curtain and place the flannel/towel set on the couch together with the bouquets. The one for Myfanwy has got a Welsh theme Cheryl put lots of Nar-scissors I think she called them in. I write the card (needing the internet to spell Myfanwy again) and then I write a card and a thank you note on Mary's.

Once I've got them arranged to my satisfaction, I pull the curtain closed and drop into the chair facing Mary's desk. Moments later I hear her keys in the front door.

'Hi Sweetie!' I say cheerfully as she walks into the room. She screams and drops her lunchbox and newspaper.

'Don't tell me,' she smirks after the eye dagger thing and a playful (?) slap across the shoulder. 'Staples, loving the new look by the way.'

I'm wearing the costume from the waist up with tracksuit bottoms and trainers below.

It's not a good look.

'Yeah a couple of them got booted by Mantis.'

'You know when I said take it easy . . .'

'Yeah see that was good advice, excellent even,' I agree quietly, 'but you're assuming that I went looking for her when I could have been just helping some poor set upon citizen and she jumped me.'

'Trousers off.'

I drop my trousers and this beacon of NHS stability and professionalism collapses in hysterics.

'I'm sorry,' she splutters after a few moments, 'cartoon boxers with that costume!' she laughs some more.

'They were on a sale.'

'Okay sit,' she says after (eventually) regaining her composure. 'Let's have a look.'

She kneels beside my leg, 'goodness your skin recovers so quickly, I'd expect it to take a week to ten days to get this far on.' She gently prods the offending patch of staples.

I manfully suppress a squeal.

'Right,' she says firmly after a moment or two of pondering. 'Everything's good apart from this section, you've got a bit of pus and discolouration, we'll have those damaged staples out, clean it up again, then stitch it back up this time.'

'Yeah?' I reply marginally less than thrilled.

'Be over in a jiffy and it'll hardly hurt at all.'

It takes a while and it is not completely without pain but I bear it stoically.

'Ok you're good,' she tells me smirking as I pull up my trackies.

'What?'

'Every time I see you on the News from now on, I'm going to remember those Boxers.

'Yeah, yeah,' suitably embarrassed I head for the door.

'So that's it then is it?' She mocks. 'Off to save the world no time to say thank you to the little nurse.'

'I saved the world yesterday and maybe instead of saying thank you, I'd opt to spend time in trying to thank you properly. Maybe by leaving something for you on the couch behind the screen.

I'm out and gone before she can react and the moral high ground is mine, yes it is!

Alsop, Rudd and associates have decent security software but I've come across it before and know how to get round it. I spend most of the afternoon and the only thing I discover is that the relationship between one of the partners and his office manager is more personal than personnel.

There's nothing that I can see that would interest Mantis and it's definitely the right office because there's a statement about the raid which boils down to damage was done but nothing was taken.

More mystery.

Then I decide to try and speak to Emma online, she's not been in for a while but I'm certain that she was genuine about me keeping in touch.

She has an online help forum (free legal advice for those who can't afford it.) I log onto it with the tablet (which always has a pay as you go Sim installed.)

HI, we spoke on your balcony, you told me to look in on you again but you're so rarely in. I type quickly.

She sends me a link almost immediately, it's a private chat

room and my software tells me it's legit.

I'd hoped we'd be able to speak. She replies. *I'm in hospital, it's so tiresome.*

Goodness, I didn't know are you alright?

Women's problems, shall I give you the details?

God no, sorry, I was aiming for polite concern.

She sends me a smiling face and a thumbs up. *What do you think about these disappearances?*

It's been going on for a while now I know that. It's not really my thing, I'm the blunt object remember.

I have a feeling that it very soon will be.

Is this connected with the two guys taken from their cells?

It is and it's no longer just the two, the others have been broken out as well.

I've seen nothing on this.

News blackout, highest level they don't want the public to panic.

What can you tell me. I ask her.

What can you tell me?

I'm sorry?

'How many people, who were they?'

About a dozen individually, mostly vagrants and down and outs then some legal types, left in a Taxi that never arrived.

There's a long pause before she replies - *Not about a dozen, exactly a dozen and that is significant. Remember what we spoke about last time and then ask yourself this. If something is dangerous, so dangerous that it's completely illegal and its ownership is disputed amongst different parts of the establishment what do you suppose happens to it? Where do you think it's kept?*

I think for a moment. *Well firstly I'd be tempted to ask why different parts of the establishment would want access to something so deadly.*

Science my boy, cutting edge, state of the art, remarkable knowledge with staggering implications. Completely unethical obviously and of course our country is at the very forefront of maintaining these standards but there are other countries out there. Countries with different agendas, different standards. Now they probably will want to look and experiment, they're sure to, so in that case . . .

We'll have a look first?

Yes.

And might one of these branches of the establishment be the military? I ask but I've already guessed the answer.

Yes but that wasn't the question I asked you was it. My question Was who looks after it, who's got it for safekeeping? Whilst the establishment argues with itself about who owns it, who should take charge? Who's looking after it?

The courts. I answer after a moment.

Yes – now remember what we talked about before - be careful please!

She attaches three praying hand symbols.

Congratulations on Barclay and Mantis by the way but this is a whole new level!

Our conversation is ended by my phone and Wil in that order.

A rather excited Wil tells me that he's got a rather wonderful new contact. The good news is that the pay is excellent, the bad news is that it's working at night.

Turns out that a local business partnership has been handing out second hand IT equipment to the more impoverished schools in the area. The partnerships IT 'expert' declared the computers safe after deleting everything and emptying the recycle bins.

When the education Authority found out they slapped *do not use* orders onto all of the machines.

Then they spoke to Wil about getting someone to thoroughly wipe the hard drives and then reconfigure them properly.

Wil knew just the guy.

I'm starting tomorrow night.

It's all actually, for once, pretty straightforward, reformat the machine and reinstall the operating systems. Caretakers let me in early evening, then out (very) early morning. The only issue is the number of machines, there are hundreds of them!

To be honest I quite enjoy the break, I take the bike and

always take the long route home.

Over the course of a fortnight I see next to nothing, a single mugging on a very late Wednesday and the police are there before I pull the bike over.

There's definitely more coppers about and there's definitely more of them that are armed. It seems like maybe Any-Man has succeeded in one thing if nothing else.

I spend my daytime going over the news channels and checking old reports. There's still no mention of the other gang members but there is more about the legal types in the taxi.

Charlie Fetherington came from an old (and very posh) family that wasn't that far removed from royalty.

Young Charlie was an athlete and ran for England under eighteens in his youth. He'd gone on to become a well respected prosecutor.

His disappearance alone had generated more headlines than the dozen vagrants put together.

In the taxi with him were two defence barristers, one who was a year from retirement having seen and done just about everything that a defence barrister could. His colleague had just qualified and was right at the start of his career.

There was a secretary as well called Jenny Jameson. The four of them were picked up from the courts and taken by taxi to their homes but none of them got there.

Several of the more lurid tabloids described the remains of the abandoned vehicle that turned up a few days later as having been torn in two, all added that there were large amounts of blood on all of the seats.

Now most of the News channels had done their own reports, looking into the people, trying to find connections and basically getting nowhere fast.

However one of the local channels had gone further than the others tying the disappearances in with a local ghostly figure called the Bagman.

The Bagman haunts an area known as Newtown bay (or Newtown bog or just the bog to the locals.) It was near here that the remains of the taxi were found and where at least three of the vagrants disappeared.

Newtown bay boils down to several acres of concrete boxes of various sizes, 1970's architecture at its very worst. There were issues from the very start, primarily flooding, they'd built it onto a floodplain with a state of the art drainage system which in a nutshell, didn't work.

As time moved on a host of other issues became more and more apparent. It seemed that the Local Authority had used the developer that gave them the lowest quote, without looking in to why it was half that of all the other bidders. The developers didn't just cut corners, they slashed them and with each year that passed the consequences became more and more apparent.

Finally following a prolonged spell of heavy rain huge cracks started to appear in the walls and great discoloured patches spread over the concrete like a rash.

A surveying team declared that concrete cancer was the issue and that the whole site was affected. In essence the steel used to reinforce the concrete on the inside had started to rust and this set off a chemical reaction within the concrete itself which meant that the whole site was now unsafe and needed to be pulled down.

As residents were re-homed in tower blocks, all of the legal disputes began.

Numerous investment companies and pension schemes had large amounts of money tied up in Newtown Bay and the original developers had gone bankrupt.

So the initial scramble was for everyone just to get their money back.

Then the Thames barrier was finished and gave proper control of water levels and suddenly Newtown bay looked less like a failed experiment and more like prime investment potential, several acres in the heart of the capital. A bid was put in to the EU and a fabulous grant was the result all that remained was to establish who owned what.

The original developers however were as lax at their paperwork as they were at following building regulations and to further complicate matters a fire at their offices shortly before they declared insolvency, destroyed what records they'd made.

The result was Newtown bay was left in limbo and left to rot as the legal disputes slid into stalemate.

A security company took over the site but rather than patrolling it, they simply left half a dozen Rottweiler's the size of pit ponies roaming the site.

Any of the local youngsters that were attacked by the dogs were simply told that they shouldn't have been there. The whole of the site was after all fenced and sign-posted as private property.

The site as well as containing over a hundred houses and a dozen shops, also had a school, a clinic and even a small civic centre with its own courtroom.

So the news reports are kept online on the stations website I click onto the relevant ones one at a time and watch them through.

Now Roger the channel anchor is clearly a bit of a lad, he's seeing his stint with LDT news as an audition for the BBC or maybe even Hollywood.

He's done his piece on 'The bagman' on an abandoned railway siding. One of the production crew has clearly started a fire downwind of him as plumes of white smoke roll along the ground behind him like mist or fog. They've put a moonlight filter on the lens so Roger looks like he's on the set of Hammer's latest offering.

'So Micky,' Roger thrusts the microphone under the chin of the nearest of a large circle of exceptionally scruffy teenagers. Roger's got one eye on the camera mind. 'Why do you all call him 'The bagman?''

'See when he does them in, he crushes them or he cuts their throats like.' Micky draws a finger along his throat and clicks his teeth. Then as they're gagging on the ground he ties their wrists to their ankles then he slings them up on his shoulder like a bag.

All the youngsters nod and agree loudly.

'And he's got a cape like batman.' Another shouts and all agree vocally again.

'A cape like Batman?' Roger points the microphone at the lads whilst he makes his eyes large for the camera.

'And wings on his head.' Another says to more vocal agreement.

'Wings on his head?' Roger's not so sure about this one. 'Are you sure?'

'Aye, they flap when he walks.' Another says to more of the

same.

'What, does he take off?' Rog says waving the microphone backwards and forwards. 'Can he fly?'

A dozen silent kids look at Roger like he's an idiot.

'Well do you know where he goes?' Roger tries to regain the initiative.

All the kids shake their heads apart from one who holds his hand up like he's in class.

Instantly all of the others turn on him and shout him down as he starts to speak.

'You don't know nuthin' Tommy.'

'Thick Tommy.'

'Stupid Tommy.'

The more he tries to speak the more he's shouted down.

Tommy clearly has issues, the way he holds his head, his speech is slurred, he's clearly a lot older than the rest of them.

But . . .

There's proper outrage in his eyes and expression, it comes of knowing the truth when others are laughing at you in their disbelief.

Like the little boy that saw Mantis and his parents didn't believe him.

Tommy knows something and that means these youngsters

have seen it too. If you listen to what they say and you don't believe them, then what they say doesn't make sense. Wings on top of his head, flapping when he walks, nonsense right?

Well that depends on your starting point, if you're starting point is that they are honest and that they're trying to describe something that they've seen. Seen it but not fully understood it then it all falls into place and everything that Emma's told me is as real as it is deadly.

I have to find Tommy.

The initial report was filmed on a hill overlooking Newtown bay, itself a rundown area, a labyrinth of tiny detached houses in several long parallel streets that lead to nowhere. There's not many high buildings about so initially I'm not sure how to get there.

If I just turn up as Stephen Bishop nobody is likely to want to talk to me, they're more likely to talk to Any-Man but I can't really walk through the streets in costume.

My problem is solved rather elegantly by London herself. A proper old fashioned fog, a real pea souper.

I reach the railway siding in good time but there's no kids about. The fog adds to the atmosphere rather wonderfully, I catch sight of my mask as it looms out of the fog in the wing mirror of a wrecked Cortina. It makes me jump, it has to be said fog makes a great backdrop, especially when you find yourself in the middle of a ghost story.

The Newtown fence is at the end of the embankment but I know that because I looked at Google maps rather than I can actually see it. Behind me the streets to nowhere run in long parallel lines, there are broken windows and graffiti and lots of boarded up windows. At a guess I'd say half the houses here are unoccupied, where else in London can you say that? I climb onto the roof of a derelict hairdressing salon at the very end of one row.

I look at the houses and am surprised by the state of the roofs. Slate's missing, lead strips ripped away, sometimes it's hard to believe that its 2022.

I'm guessing the kids will be inside on the consoles, it's a lousy night. I sit with my back to a chimney looking down at the battered little houses below and run over things in my mind, I'm pretty certain that I know what's going on and I think I know who's behind it and why but . . ?

As if on cue I hear voices in the fog on the embankment.
'We told you Tommy but you never listen.'
'Tommy's thick that's why?'

I jump from the roof and land deliberately noisily then stomp towards them.

There's seven of them and their faces are a picture.

'Tommy I need a word, I won't harm any of you I promise.'

As one they gape back at me, mouths like tunnels.

'You're not the Vigilante,' the tallest one scoffs after a few moments, 'he's well bigger than you, your just wearing a mask.'

I grab his belt with my right hand and lift him up over my head. 'Do you want to see how far I can throw you?'

'NO, NO, please NO!' The lad screams, 'you're him, you're him.'

I lower him to the ground.

'We done nuthin' mister!' Another lad shouts and the rest agree loudly.

'I'm not after any of you boy's, I just want a word with Tommy.'

Tommy's still stood with the same thunderstruck expression.

'What do you want him for?'

'Tommy's thick!'

'Tommy knows nuthin' about nuthin''

'Well my super senses tell me that Tommy is the only one here who knows what I need to know. He's the only one here who can help me.'

The seven go back to their tunnel impersonations.

'So then, Bye lads!' I fold my arms across my chest.

They stare at me blankly for a few moments before taking the hint and scurrying away leaving just me with Tommy. 'Are you going to beat me up?' He looks terrified. 'I ain't done nuthin' honest.'

I lean forward and place my hand on his shoulder. 'You're not in any trouble Tommy I promise you, I really do need your help.'

He nods slowly but still looks terrified.

'With me.' I nod towards the back of the embankment and set off towards it, Tommy walks alongside, his knees knocking like a condemned man.

As we approach the fence the site becomes more open and a swirling wind thins the fog, I can soon see that nobody is in earshot so I stop.

'Tommy I saw you on the news and I could see at once that you knew something, you wanted to speak but nobody was letting you.'

His demeanour changes in a flash, suddenly he's all smiles. 'I tried to tell the police but they wouldn't believe me then I tries to tell the news man and he wouldn't listen.'

'I'm listening Tommy, I believe that there is a Bagman and I'm sure he lives in the bay somewhere.'

'You're after him aren't you?' Tommy stamps his feet and his mouth drops open. 'You're going to stop him.'

'I have to Tommy.'

His face breaks into an enormous grin, 'what goes around

273

comes around, gran always tells me that. He's cruel and he's horrible.'

'Tell me Tommy.'

'The man, the rich one on the news.'

'The prosecutor?'

'He was crying like a baby, his voice was all high, he sounded like he were squeaking. The Bagman just broke him, snapped him with his hands and there was a girl . . .' Tommy looks away clearly embarrassed.

'Go on Tommy.'

'I wanted to help her really I did, she was having some kind of attack like Asthma but sobbing and screaming at the same time, it was such a noise but I was too scared.'

'Tommy you'd just have got yourself killed.'

'I told em', I did what they say to do, if you can't help, get help but nobody would listen.'

'Tommy where did this happen? I ask him quietly. 'Where did you see him?'

Tommy points towards the fence, as we approach I see a huge hole in it.

'Blimey you could drive a car through that, at least the Rottweiler's will have gone.'

'All the Rotties are dead,' Tommy tells me cheerfully. 'Can't you smell it?'

There is a bit of a smell to be honest but it's over the whole embankment not just here.

We scramble through the hole and Tommy leads me past an old broken bench to what was once a kiddies play area. Everything is broken and covered in graffiti, the slide, the swing, the lot.

Slap bang in the middle of the park is the corpse of what looks at first like a pony on its side. Even with its head squashed flat it's the biggest Rottweiler that I've ever seen.

'God above what the hell did he do to that?' I gasp genuinely startled.

'That's how the ghost does them, sometimes he just breaks them up with his hands other times he smashes them with his hammer.'

'He's got a hammer?'

'Aye, like Thor.'

'Outstanding!'

We head to the end of the path looking down the hill towards the estate.

It's overgrown, derelict and frankly it stinks, the smell is worse by here and it makes me cough.

'Think this is bad, wait till you get close, most can't stick it.'

I nod, looking around the path.

Somebody has vomited here recently and there's blood as well. Then there's a shoe, I pick it up, now I'm no fashion expert but even I can see that it's expensive, really expensive. Inside, the feeble light of the low sun peeking through the fog is enough to show me the logo *Lloyds handmade.* There's money here as well and a fountain pen.

'Here, finder's fee, you've earned it,' I hand the cash to Tommy.

'Gran says I'm not to take money from people and if I finds it I should hand it in cos them that lost it will want it back.' I stuff the money into his shirt pocket. 'She's quite right too.' I tell him. 'Under normal circumstances but these are not normal circumstances besides this fella has no use for his money anymore.'

'Who's was it.'

'Charlie Fetherington,' I tell him holding up the monogrammed fountain pen.

'Right Tommy you've done bloody marvellously.' I put my hand on his shoulder.

'Don't you want to know where the ghost lives?'

'Oh I'm pretty certain I've worked it out my friend.' I answer quietly, 'I'm betting he'll be in there.' I point to a large building near the main entrance to the site.'

'How did you know?' Tommy's suitably impressed.

'Well those same super senses of mine that told me I could trust you, told me he'd be in there.'

'Can I really keep this cash?'

'Absolutely, spend it on you or your gran and if anyone's got a problem with that you tell them that they've got to take it up with me.'

Tommy laughs.

'One final thing my friend, that circle in the ground behind those buildings,' I point. 'What's going on there?'

'It was a tunnel for the subway but the money ran out, all the machinery is there around it they just left it. It's real dangerous, bloody great hole they reckon it's a hundred feet straight down. We reckon that's how he escaped, cos it's right by where he lives.'

'Escaped from where?'

'From Hell!'

'Okay, with me.' I tell him after a few moments.

'Where we going?' He shouts, hurrying after me.

'You're going home.' I tell him when we reach the fence.

'But I want to help.'

'Too dangerous, besides there's one more thing I want you to do for me.'

'What? Anything.'

'You know how the police didn't want to talk to you before?'

'They said I was making it up and next time they'd do me for wasting their time.

'Most coppers are alright Tommy, they want to make a difference but there's far too much work and not enough of them.'

Tommy nods.

'Well Tommy tomorrow the coppers will be wanting to talk

to you. When they do you tell them that I told you to give them this.' I hand him the fountain pen. 'And take them to that building, say Charlie Fetherington's killer was in there and I went in after him.'

'How will they know?'

'I've sent an email to a lady that the police *will* listen to telling her that a local lad called Tommy knows where the Bagman lives and he's going to show me. She won't get it until seven tomorrow morning. Do you have a mobile?'

Tommy nods.

'Number?'

He recites it slowly concentrating hard.

'Ok, I've got it, if the plan changes I'll call you.'

'Aren't you going to write it down?'

'I'm good with numbers, super senses mate, now you go straight home, I'll wait for five, anything happens just yell.'

Tommy sets off his head down in determination, I climb the fence to watch and only leave when I'm sure he's safe.

I walk back quietly to the bay, the sun's starting to set now as the fog just slides away into nowhere like its done its job. Approaching the buildings the smell is dreadful, I'm reminded of my dream, the smell in the room and corridor but that was the smell of blood this is decay. It's as if the rot and the ruin of the outside of the buildings is a reflection of the death and decay within.

I wander to the hole first, its wonderfully quiet, I'm not far from the centre of the capital but I could be on the moon. Half a dozen pipistrels play tag around the roof of the court building which seems to be the source of the dreadful smell.

The hole is huge and there's an enormous machine the size of a car beside it. It looks like a compressed locomotive, it's covered in rust, muck and spiders webs.
On the road beside it is a woman's skirt, white, clean and pressed but splashed with blood.

I shudder and walk towards the court building and the second I open the double door I know I've found what I'm looking for.

I can't describe the smell to you; it's like a punch in the face. In seconds my eyes are streaming and the back of my nose and throat are on fire.

I walk into reception, there's an inch and a half of dust over everything except the middle of the floor where the same feet has dragged many through. Shoes, slippers, torn trousers, a jacket, a coat and there's blood stains all over, like the graffiti it covers.

I draw the metal bar from the back of my belt, gripping it firmly I turn down the corridor, my feet crunching on the broken glass as I gag at the smell.

A sign on the wall says The presiding judge today is- and beneath his name is made up of little plastic crème coloured letters that slide into a groove and spell out the name that I expected or maybe that's suspected I'd see.

Tommy was right, it *is* a ghost, not in the sense that Tommy or his friends meant but there is a ghost that haunts this building, a ghost I must confront tonight.

The main court is at the end of the corridor behind two closed double doors.

I steady myself and even pray, before I push the doors open and step into hell.

To the death – Chapter fourteen.

If I was to describe it to you I'd say think computer game, those dark shoot em' ups with zombies.

The first thing you see in the darkened court room is the jury. On one long bench are twelve men and women good and true and each and everyone of them is long dead. They sit in the remains of their clothes crawling with maggots and insects, they're bodies all in various stages of decay. Rats scramble over them and through them as if they're playing tag.
The sight of it and the smell of it is beyond appalling. Despite the lateness of the day there's a million flies in the room like a busy cloud swarming over them.
To their left, sat in chairs behind their respective tables, dressed in their robes are the judiciary or their remains. I recognise Charlie and Jenny who both died looking completely terrified, it's impossible to look at them without feeling so sorry for them.

Their bodies have been propped up and posed, like manikins in a shop window.

The whole thing is the most vile and hideous travesty of a

court that you can imagine but it is not entirely unexpected, not once I put the pieces together.

I cough to clear my throat and try to speak loudly and clearly even though the stench of the room makes me want to wretch.
'I had a look at your Wikipedia page. His honour Christopher William Henry Blackmoor. Stand out judge, committed humanist completely determined to make his life count for something, to make a difference and to leave the world a better place. Christopher believed with a passion that all men were fundamentally good . . .'

I stop, there's a buzz and a hum over the speakers, there's a circuit, a hearing loop in the court. It's normally to allow those with hearing aids in the court to hear what's being said.
But he's playing music, it's so faint that I can hardly hear it and I can't quite place it.

'That being so Christopher was determined to use his intellect and compassion wisely. He wouldn't just throw long sentences at people he'd try and reform them, he'd give people a chance. Some called him the *just* judge, the fair judge others called him naive and fool. He spent a lifetime in service, he didn't get the promotions or advancement you'd expect but he carried on undaunted.'

The music begins to swell, it's the introduction to a pop song, what's it called now? Lovely looking girl, dusky skin, fair hair what the hell's her name?
'Then on his last day in court, after a lifetime of service the day before he was due to retire he got the news that his only child, a much loved daughter, had been shot dead by a career criminal. A criminal that was free because Christopher had given him the benefit of the doubt six months before. He let him walk on a technicality rather than banging him up inside again.'

I walk our streets and search our places

Seeking you, calling, searching those faces

I don't know why this is happening or what i've done wrong

I just know that everything is empty, now that you're gone.

The singer's rich, wonderful voice could not be more out of place but I remember the song now and I can see what he sees in the lyrics.
'Walking is so difficult isn't it?' I say to him, watching his

shadow detach itself from the others at the front of the court. 'Every step is too much effort, too much energy, your muscles suddenly have twelve times their strength and power, it's all you can do to contain it. It's like walking on a trampoline or a bouncy castle.' I tell him as his red and black robes swirl like a cape around him and his wig flaps on his head like the wings of a bird.

'Something you appear to have mastered,' he replies calmly, without a hint of the madness within. 'You'll have an alter-ego to care about and maintain no doubt.'

I nod.

'No such worries.' He tells me pointing at himself. 'It's hard enough to be me, I can't allow anyone else to get in the way.

There's no laugher, no living, no life without you

I don't know how to get by, I don't know what to do

A life without living is just no life at all

You won't come when i'm looking, you don't answer my call

'Emma told me that she was a remarkable young woman, tell me about her.' I reply quietly.

'We used to call her our sunshine, we were late to have children . . .?'

'Your wife?'

'Died eighteen months ago, Dementia.'

'I'm Sorry.'

'Eleanor nursed her for as long as she could, I worked, Eleanor kept house and looked after her Mum. We were a team.'

'Emma said she was special.'

'She was remarkable, she could have . . . she would have . . .' Suddenly he just looks like a tired old man. 'She was everything, she kept me going, kept my head high.'

'She sounds wonderful.'

He nods quickly, tears streaming down his face. 'She was everything, no Father could ask for more.'

Wherever I look your just never there

I try and I try it's all so unfair

I'm hunting and searching, looking high, looking low

You're out of my life babe, where did you go?

What did I do, what did I do?

What did I do, oh what did I do?

The chorus kicks in and his mood changes in a flash abruptly he's smiling away, staring into space and mumbling softly to himself.

'So how do you want to do this?' I ask with a sigh, tightening my grip on the bar.

'Must we?'

'Tell me about the others then.'

He nods with a relieved smile. 'Well Julian was first, Julian Rendle QC, he made sure that I had to go and identify the body. There's normally some discretion you understand but Julian had hated my methods for a lifetime and this was a gift. He stepped in personally. 'Let him see the consequences of his actions for himself he told the police chief.'

I shake my head, 'what a bastard!'

'Twelve bore point blank in the face, my little girl.'

I shake my head again.

'When I found out that he'd insisted that I see it for myself I went around to see him. Julian's done really well for himself, huge house in the country real, Lord of the manor. He's stood there in his suit and wellies at the bottom of the garden. Didn't even look up as I approached, you've only got yourself to blame Christopher, that's what he said. Just a shame that you had to learn your lesson too late, if you'd learnt it before retirement you might even have been able to

do some good for once.'
'What a complete . . ! I'm so sorry Christopher.'

Without you i'm dying, without you I'll fall

You were my reason, my hope and my all

Now I've only ashes and memory and empty endless days

I'm left with a heart that is broken and a lifetime to pay

'Julian had a brand new macerator in a drainage ditch at the
bottom of his garden. Have you ever seen one?'
'Machinery that cuts and grinds up solids to make slurry,
there was one on a cop show I watched once.' I answer after
a moment.
He nods, 'Julian was there chucking all his waste into it, it
makes a terrible noise. This is how you deal with rubbish
Christopher, he said. This is how you deal with vermin. The
paramedic took your daughters face into the ambulance in a
carrier bag that's what happens when you pander to filth!'

'What did you do?' I gasp.
He looks at me and a slow smile pulls at the corner of his mouth as he raises one eyebrow.
'The macerator?' I ask with a groan.
'Seemed a shame to waste it.' He tells me.

Wherever I look your just never there

I try and I try it's all so unfair

I'm hunting and searching, looking high, looking low

You're out of my life babe, where did you go?

What did I do, what did I do?

What did I do, oh what did I do?

The record finishes with a click.

'So he was your first?'
'Yes, it was just me then. Julian was a bully, a bear of a man, I'd never hit anyone in my life so he didn't see it coming.'
'So then you thought if you could deal with him . . .'

'I remembered the chemical in the stores, I'd not been involved but I knew the gist of its back story.

'Do you know where it came from?'

He shakes his head, 'only what it was supposed to do. We all thought it was a ridiculous fuss over some chemicals in an attaché case I just walked into the storeroom and injected myself. There's always drug paraphernalia in there.'

'Any side effects,' I ask him quickly, 'you've clearly not suffered amnesia.'

'It was the likelihood of mental damage that triggered the court order that prohibited its use but I've had no side effects at all. I can remember everything and you can see for yourself that my sanity has been un-effected.'

'Right,' I reply quietly looking around at his court. 'What about the others, the jury?'

'The jury were chosen, that's how it works.'

'But they had lives of their own.'

'I know, I'm not without compassion, I chose only vagrants and drug addicts, those who had already given up on life.'

'That one on the end, closest to you, going by the clothes that's a girl, probably the same age as yours was. In all likelihood she's got a Father out there somewhere, waiting and worrying, going through all that you did.'

He raises his eyebrows and nods, 'you're probably right it's true but sacrifices have to be made.'

'Yeah but that's hardly our call is it?'

'I'm sensing you don't approve.'

'Judge look around you, it's a chamber of horrors, how can this be the answer?'

'What the hell do you think we're dealing with? Horror is precisely what's out there. You fight fire with fire boy.' He answers throwing up his arms. 'I spent a lifetime giving them the benefit of the doubt, turning the other cheek, going the extra mile and for what? My daughter's ashes in a jar.'

But if you use their methods how are you any better?'

'Seriously?' He scoffs, 'that's the argument that you're going to use, is that what you'll bring before me.'

He turns his back on me and heads for the judges seat. 'You sit there,' he points to a chair between the dead judiciary.

'I'm good standing thanks.' I tell him glancing at the corpses.

He pulls his seat noisily out from behind its bench, I notice a polo mallet lying across it.

As he sits, I get my first properly good look at him, although he's slightly further back than earlier.

The courtroom is dark because the blinds are drawn but a tear in one throws a band of light onto the judge's station. His robes are torn and filthy with dried blood, he's dishevelled but for all that you can practically feel the strength and power in him. He's shuffling papers on his desk but they're all just blank sheets.

His face is bruised and battered.

'What happened to your face?'

He looks up, 'Durand's attack dog of course, I'm assuming that you'll have encountered Gabriel Durand and his cronies by now.'

'Can't say I've had the pleasure.'

'It's no pleasure I assure you,' he sighs bundling up the papers. 'Now to business. The gang that killed my little girl were captured by you, they were in the act of robbing a bank I believe?'

'Yes that is correct.'

'And you're way of dealing with these murderers was a single slap, don't deny it I've seen the CCTV.'

'I've no intention of denying it and if you've seen the CCTV as you claim then you'll know damn well that there was a hostage and they had shotguns. I had to put them down as quickly as possible.'

'And you thought that a slap was adequate retribution?'

'I'm not concerned about retribution, that's what the courts are for, what people like you are for. I was only interested in rendering them harmless as quickly and as safely as possible.'

He stares at me silently, then his smile grows. 'Oh my dear boy, I was so sure that this would become unpleasant and you and I would have to come to blows. I hardly dared hope that I might be able to reason with you and bring you around but you're halfway there already.'

'I'm sorry?'

'Just bear with me, look you would agree that the system is broken would you not?'

'It certainly isn't working the way that it is supposed to or that it was intended to but that's down to chronic under investment and resourcing.'

'Oh my dear boy don't be so dense, the reasons are gloriously irrelevant. You and I are pawns, we play the hand we're dealt rather than wishing for better cards. The system is broken right?'

'Yes.'

'The job you do would normally be done by the police am I correct?'

'Yes of course but there aren't enough of them and . . .'

'Cards boy! It's the cards that you have that we're talking about not the cards you want, how many times?' He sighs and adjusts his wig. 'You are doing their job, am I correct?'

'Yes.'

'Because they're failing to do it?'

'Sometimes, yes.'

'And when you work you are dispassionate, you're not interested in dishing out justice your simply trying to keep people safe.'

'Well . . . broadly yes I guess.'

'Bit of hesitation there young man and all of a sudden you're not sounding quite so convinced.'

'It isn't always that simple is it?'

'No it isn't is it?' He gives me a wicked smile. 'They were just bank robbers with a hostage, no more? You didn't know their history, you didn't know what they had done?'

'I knew there had been a bank robbery a few weeks before and I knew that a girl had died. I knew it was a possibility but I couldn't be certain.'

'Answer me honestly, if you had been sure it was them, if you'd known which of them it was, would it have just been a slap?'

I stare at him for long moments; he just looks calm and reasonable, every inch the judge. 'I'd have walloped him properly, I'd have hurt him.'

Christopher claps his hands and grins manically at the rotting prosecutor before returning his attention to me.

'And honestly again if you please, has there been times that you've stepped over the lines that you draw for yourself?'

'Yes.'

'Elaborate.'

'A wife beater, huge guy with a hammer, his wife was the size of a ten year old, a bear with a mouse.'

'Any more?'

'A guy pulled a kid from her Mother's car, dragged her up a back lane, punched her when she tried to escape.'

'So you hurt both of these men, you really hurt them?'

'Yes.'

'So it wasn't just about making them stop, it wasn't

dispassionate, you wanted to dish out justice as well?'

'I didn't think about it, I don't think you have time to consider it. We're human, we're not perfect, sometimes you lose your temper.'

'So not superhuman at all then?'

'In that sense clearly not.'

'Okay let's try another angle, you've crossed swords with a good number now, how do you react when you see the same faces?'

'You mean when I catch someone doing again what I nailed them for doing before?'

'Exactly.'

'There's only been a few, a mugger down by the canal bridge and a house breaker on a nearby estate.

'So you caught them, gave them a hiding, then sometime later they're doing the same thing in exactly the same neck of the woods.'

'Pretty much.'

'Annoying?'

'Yes, really annoying.'

'So you gave them a second hiding, and no doubt this was worse than the first. Am I right?'

'Pretty much.'

'So then the truth of this is simple, you claim to be dispassionate, somebody who's just trying to make it all stop. But in reality you're just as interested in dishing out justice.'

I can't think of an answer.

'See, I used to think that people can change and you're absolutely right I used to bend over backwards and do all that the law would allow to give them every chance but . . .'

'Hold on,' I interrupt as a thought strikes me. 'Are you telling me that in all your time, in all your cases that there were none. No rehabilitation, no lives turned around? Are you telling me that it was all one way traffic?'

He pauses for a long moment. 'There were some I concede, there was some success but for most compassion was seen only as a sign of weakness. An opportunity only, for taking advantage.'

'How many?'

'This is not about numbers boy.'

'You made it about numbers judge, the one that beat his wife, the one that stole the girl. How many, what proportion?'

'Not enough to justify . . .'

'What happened to Eleanor? Judge nothing could be able to justify that. There is no justification, some people are just wrong it's in their DNA, there's no changing them.'

'Precisely, that's exactly the point . . .'

'But you can't tar everyone else with the same brush.'

'The end justifies the means.'

'The end does not justify the means and here's the proof.' I point to the body of a young woman, slumped at a desk with a pen jammed into her hand. 'Can you tell me her name Judge?'

'No, I'm afraid I can't,' he replies after a long moment of consideration.

'Jenny Jameson, not a vagrant, not a druggie, she hadn't given up on life, she looked after her Dad who had Parkinson's. Legal Secretary according to her profile. What did you do, steal the cab and wait outside the court.

'Nobody ever looks at the drivers. They park around the back and pop into the kitchen for a cuppa. They think we don't know. '

So you stole the cab and picked them up around the front.' He nods, 'what of it?'

'You were seen by some kids on the estate as you finished them, Jenny was hysterical, begging you, pleading with you, screaming.'

'She had a panic attack, you should have seen the state she got into and heard the noise that she made. It was a kindness in the end.'

'It was not a kindness, it was never a kindness, it was another man's daughter as loved, special and precious as your own. Everything she was, everything she could have been, the children she might have had, all stolen away from her by you.'

He sighs sadly, loud and long, 'you're not getting this are

you?'

'What happened to your daughter was disgraceful, an appalling act by the very lowest of humanity but if your justice, your answer, is to do exactly the same thing to another man's daughter, another innocent, then you've lost before you start. You've become the very thing that you're setting out to fight.' I look around his court, 'this is a travesty, how can this be justice?'

'Justice has to be seen to . . .'

'Christopher stop, look at it, this is madness.'

He rises slowly from his chair, 'you and I could have worked together, we could have shown the city, shown the world, proper effective justice. Justice that worked, zero tolerance.'

'Justice that took no prisoners, me going out and bringing them in to you . . .'

'And me administering justice with an iron hand, Justice that is respected, justice that is feared.'

'With only ever one verdict? That's not zero tolerance, that's zero justice.'

'Oh my dear boy,' he winces shaking his head. 'Stop and think for a moment, you've clearly got a brain why not give it a chance?' Look it won't be permanent, it won't always be this way. I agree it's all a tad ghastly to begin with but once people see the consequences, once they know what's going to happen, they'll *all* start to tow the line. It's like parking orders, they begin as letters asking nicely, everybody ignores them so they become points on your licence and a harsh fine. It's then that they start to become effective. Once people know that there will be consequences and that those consequences will hurt, then they'll get into line. The people are sheep my boy, how do you suppose that those muppets in Downing street are able to control them and to get away with all that they do? We start heavy and hard and yes it will be gruesome for a while longer but it will work as long as we hold our nerve.'

He believes every word he's saying and I know that there's no convincing him otherwise. I shake my head.

'We're not going to agree are we?' He snaps, 'Which means there will be unpleasantness.

'I fear so.'

'Then I ask one thing of you.'

'Go on.'

'If we're to fight it must be to the death, be assured that I know now absolutely that I cannot let you live and given the chance I will end you quickly and with compassion. You caught them, you took their freedom and got them incarcerated so that I could finish the job properly. I am and will always be grateful to you for that. Your end if it comes to me to deliver it will be quick, I ask the same from you.'

'Judge you need help.'

'That is what I feared you'd say, your help will see me in over-sized nappies in an institution drugged out of my mind and waiting for the end. I've seen one I love die like that don't you dare offer that to me as a mercy.'

I nod slowly.

'Thank you.' He rises slowly keeping his eyes on me. 'There has to be justice boy.'

'Some would say that true justice rarely comes here but it always comes.'

'The afterlife? Oh please, I'm a little too old for fairy tales.'

'That's right you're a humanist aren't you? Does that mean that you believe in nothing then?'

'What and you do?'

'I believe that there is a hell of a lot more to this world than what we can see.'

'There's no salvation for me boy, there's no appeal to faith.'

'What if it was the only way that you'd ever be able to see them again?'

He stares at me for a long moment, you can almost see the wheels turning.

Then without warning he's flying towards me, his first punch catches me unawares and for the first time it's a proper punch. I stagger backwards seeing stars, he catches me twice more in the face, despite the padding of the mask I'm reeling. He's every bit as strong as I am if not more and he's quick.

Then I'm on my knees, trying to get back up, for a second he's gone and I can't see him. Then he's racing back at me with the polo hammer.

There's an almighty bang and then agony as his hammer slams into the side of my head and blackness overwhelms me as I sink to the floor.

Many thanks for reading, I hope you enjoyed this book. If you want to get in touch please do, I'm on –
davidoverland1@aol.co.uk

If you enjoyed this book please leave a review on Amazon or Goodreads if you can, it honestly makes all the difference to us.

Printed in Great Britain
by Amazon